BT26.95

'BRARY

:ALL

D0065519

DATE DUE

AUG 2 8 1999	JUN 0 5 2001
OCT 1 2 1999	JUN 0 5 2004
OCT 1 6 1999	
DEC 0 8 1999	MAR 2 0 2005
JAN 1 8 2000	NOV 1 6 2011
FEB 2 0 2000	
MAR 1 0 2000	
MAY 1 5 2003	

Falling
to
earth

Falling
to earth

a novel

elizabeth brownrigg

Firebrand
Books

Book design by Jane MacDonald
Cover design by Nightwood

Printed on acid-free paper in the U.S. by McNaughton & Gunn

10 9 8 7 6 5 4 3 2 1

Library of Congress Cataloging-in-Publication Data

Brownrigg, Elizabeth, 1952–
    Falling to earth : a novel / by Elizabeth Brownrigg.
        p.   cm.
    ISBN 1–56341–101–6 (alk. paper). — ISBN 1–56341–100–8 (pbk. : alk. paper)
    I. Title.
    PS3552.R7865F35   1998
813' .54—dc21   98–33588
                                                                            CIP

Acknowledgments

I would like to thank my teachers: Joyce Johnson, Joan Silber, Chuck Wachtel, and Mary Elsie Robertson.

Thanks also to the readers of this novel in its early stages for their invaluable criticism: Teresa Ortega, Angela Williams, Catherine Nicholson, Amber Taylor, Kate Green, Jody Eimers, Melissa Delbridge, Jocelyn Lieu, Dale Neal, Susan Sterling, Helen Fremont, Nan Cuba, Susan Ballinger, Wynn Cherry, Barb Brooks, and Ronna Dornsife.

And thanks to Nancy Bereano, for opening the door.

for Dee

This is a story about doppelgängers and angels and the difference between heaven and hell.

The story begins at a cabin in the Blue Ridge. I lived in the city, but I went up to the mountains for a couple of weeks every summer to swim and fish and read long, bad novels that I would be embarrassed to be seen with down in the valley.

On an August day around noon, I put on my bathing suit and followed the path down to the river. I walked into the water up to my chest. The river was only slightly cooler than the hot summer air around it. I leaned back and floated in the still water. There was something on a sycamore branch far above my head. I was staring at whatever it was upside down, so I paddled myself around to get a better look. It was a woman with red hair who was wearing a white nightgown. She had wings.

"Jesus Christ!" I floundered to my feet.

"Not quite," she said.

"Who the hell are you?"

"You remember me."

I stood in the chest-high water and gawked.

"You owe me," she said.

"What?"

"You gave me your soul."

"What?"

"A bargain is a bargain," she said.

I decided to stop saying *what*. The figure in the tree crossed her arms and waited for me to say something new. I caught at the faint wisps of a memory.

When I was a little girl, I had an imaginary friend whose name was Pinky. I also had a guardian angel named Phoebe, who was different from Pinky because Phoebe was real and Pinky was only imaginary.

I told my best friend Robin about Pinky, but I didn't tell her about Phoebe. Robin didn't really have an imaginary friend, but she pretended to. I remembered an afternoon when Pinky and Robin and I played in the hot sun of the backyard while Phoebe watched from under the dogwood. Phoebe had red hair and she wore a white nightgown. Her wings moved slowly back and forth in the heat as she cooled herself, like a butterfly. Robin and I were spinning hula hoops in wild gyrations around our hips. The hula hoops went down, down, until they slipped past our ankles and fluttered to rest. We fell on the wet grass, laughing, grey insects popping up around us. Then we practiced our somersaults until we were dizzy and the sky spun like a hula hoop above our heads. I told Robin she was my very best friend in the whole wide world. Phoebe smiled at me from underneath the dogwood tree.

I liked my guardian angel much better than I liked Jesus and God His Father and the Holy Spirit, who was an expressionless bird. The Holy Spirit was sinister. God looked angry. He was also always watching me, just like my parents. I didn't think it was Eve's fault that Adam was a liar. I couldn't understand why snakes were supposed to be bad, and why the statue of Mary in the corner of the church was stepping on one. The guardian angel was the friendliest person in heaven. The rest of them would turn on you the minute you made a mistake.

In confession, I said the same thing every time: "Bless me, Father, for I have sinned. I had bad thoughts about my sister." I wished my guardian angel would do a bit more about protecting me from my big sister, who thought she was God and should watch everything I did. I wished Phoebe would stab her or make her go blind, but apparently guardian angels weren't supposed to do things like that. This seemed like poor planning to me. If Phoebe would just get rid of my sister, she wouldn't have to protect me from her anymore.

When Robin and I finished playing, she went back home and Pinky walked alongside me into the house. I forgot about Pinky as I walked through the kitchen, so she disappeared. Phoebe hovered right outside the window. I went upstairs, and she flew into my bedroom window. She sat in the rocking chair in the corner. I settled down onto my bed with *The Golden Book of Beetles*. Beetles came in all different colors and sizes and shapes and my sister hated them, which was another point in their favor.

"Look, Phoebe," I said, and I showed her a picture of a rhinoceros beetle. Phoebe looked at the beetle and nodded. Outside my bedroom window, in the trees, the cicadas buzzed. Their translucent brown shells were stuck to the bark of the dogwood tree in our yard. I thought they returned to their shells at night because my father told me, "That's the cicada's house." I played a trick on the cicadas by moving their houses so they wouldn't be able to find them when they were through buzzing for the day and wanted to go to sleep.

"I remember you," I said to Phoebe, up in her sycamore tree.

"Would now be a more convenient time for you to be pregnant?" she asked. "I can arrange it."

In high school I had my first sex with a boy I didn't even care that much about; the rubber slipped off while we were doing it. My period didn't come for weeks afterward. I was terrified of being pregnant. One night, the boy and I were parking, but I wouldn't let him go all the way this time. He said he had to take a leak and got out of the car. He walked behind some bushes, probably to jerk off. I sat in the passenger seat and hugged myself. I was tired of being scared.

Phoebe floated in front of the windshield. I hadn't seen her for a long time. "Oh, please, Phoebe," I said, "get me out of this one and I'll do anything."

Phoebe considered. "Anything?"

"Please. I can't stand this." I was really scared.

"I want your soul."

I was startled. I had stopped thinking I had a soul the year before, which was also the year I stopped believing in God. But then again, here was Phoebe. My soul was not something I thought I'd miss. "Take it. Please. Make me not pregnant."

"You're not pregnant," said Phoebe, and disappeared.

I never was sure whether I really had been pregnant or not. Phoebe didn't actually lie, but, as my mother might say, she had a tendency to prevaricate. At any rate, my period came the next day and for once I was glad to feel the steel bit on the end of the sanitary napkin belt digging into my rear.

"What is it you want?" I asked Phoebe from my spot in the river.

"I want you to write my stories."

"Can't you write them yourself?"

"I need somebody to put my words on paper. So they can be read."

"Just between you and God isn't good enough?"

When I said that, we both quickly glanced up at the sky to see if it would darken. Things might have grown very quiet for just a second. Phoebe looked back down at me as if nothing had happened.

"I want readers."

"Learn to type."

I lay down in the water and floated on my back. I moved my hands to make myself spin in lazy circles. At this angle, Phoebe was out of view. Until she came out of her tree and hovered so that her face was directly above mine. She said, "You know damn (we looked up at the sky again) well I can't type."

"Write them out longhand."

"No, stupid. I can't *touch* anything."

I reached for the hem of her nightgown, and my hand passed through it.

"Oh. I can't touch you either."

"How about that." Phoebe disappeared from view and went to

sulk in her tree. I stood up in the river. When I looked at her closely, I noticed that she wasn't actually on the branch, but hovering barely an inch above it. She was sitting with her legs crossed. In that position, she looked like a floating Buddha. With long red hair.

"Phoebe, aren't angels supposed to have blonde hair?"

"No," she said, still frowning. "That's not part of the uniform. We just get nightgowns, wings, and halos."

"Don't your feet get cold?"

"Of course not. I'm not in the same world as you."

"You're not?"

"It's like looking through glass."

I did feel a little sorry for Phoebe, forced to perpetually window-shop. She could never go inside the store and buy anything.

"Tell me the name of a story," I said.

She perked up and flew down out of her tree to flutter above the water. "'Pictures in the Dark.' I think it's about winter in Buffalo, New York."

"They say suicide in Buffalo is redundant," I interjected.

Phoebe ignored me. "Like I said," she continued, "picture Buffalo, snow, a small boy, nuns."

Of course. A story told by an angel would have to have religion in it. I waded out of the river to sit under Phoebe's tree. She floated above the rocks next to me.

"Want to see me walk on the water?" she said. She took off across the river to the far bank, doing a very good imitation of touching the water and getting her toes damp.

"Is that how He did it?" I called after her.

Phoebe turned around and held her finger to her lips. "*Ssshhhh.* I'm not supposed to tell." She tiptoed back from across the water. It looked like fun.

"Can you teach me to do that?"

"Sorry. Privileged information."

I pulled my knees up to my chest and shifted around. The hard stones of the shore hurt my butt. "What's the plot of your story?"

Phoebe looked perplexed.

"What's the small boy's name?" I asked.

She brightened. "Jo-Jo. His name is Jo-Jo."

"Good name," I said. "The subtitle could be 'Jo-Jo and the Snow.'"

"It's not about snow," she said. She closed her eyes and began to speak.

AT NIGHT, ALONE IN FRONT of the mirror in his room at home, little Jo-Jo framed his dark face in a white sheet. He turned his head this way and that; he pulled the sheet forward on top so that the edge shadowed his face. Sister Jo-Jo.

"Ave Maria," sang Jo-Jo softly, and raised his eyes to heaven. Somewhere downstairs somebody broke a dish, or maybe a lamp. A door slammed. Jo-Jo kept his room like a convent cell. There was nothing on the walls except a carved wooden crucifix that hung over his bed that he had bought by scrounging through sofas and chair cushions for the money and pinching a couple of bucks from his mother's purse. His single bed was neatly made. The mirror was the only difference. He didn't believe nuns were allowed to have mirrors.

With the sheet still draped over his head, he kneeled at the foot of his bed. Outside the window, the snow fell. The best thing about snow was that it made everything quiet, at least for a little while.

Jo-Jo went to parochial school. All the boys looked so sharp in their white shirts and navy blue blazers. Brown shiny shoes. Grey flannel trousers. In those clothes, they looked innocent. The nuns' starched white wimples matched the boys' shirts. Jo-Jo liked contrasts: the black and white of the sisters' outfits, the blue and white of the boys'. The crack of the ruler coming down on a bad boy's knuckles. Jo-Jo even liked the hard discipline. It meant order. It meant he knew what was going to happen next, as opposed to home, where who knew who was going to be drunk or messed up or simply not there.

One day, Jo-Jo opened the glass French doors that led out onto the back lawn of the school and started walking, not paying much attention to where he was going, and stumbled on a nun hiding behind a shed, smoking a cigarette. She was hunched over her treasure, the ember glowing brightly when she inhaled. He backed away until he reached the doors, opening them as silently as he could.

Nuns didn't smoke. People outside the school, people out in the rough world smoked, but this was a safe place of sharp contrasts and sharp discipline, of denial of the body.

He started to look around him more closely. The smoke of the cigarette made a rift in this otherworldly world. He saw the priest gorge himself on sweet rolls at breakfast. He smelled the stale smoke on the sister's habit when he went by her on his way to class. He saw the hands of two young nuns brush, not quite by accident. He knew what was up. And the secret desire he hadn't told himself about, for those other boys in starched white and dark blue, that was real too, just as real as the smoke of a cigarette.

"Hey fag," a boy whispered behind him in class. "Hey fag, you're a fag just like Father Petroni." So Jo-Jo started to watch Father Petroni. Him too? Father Petroni's voice was soft, like a bird's wing. He ate too many sweet rolls; the folds of his chin bore a light grey stubble. Jo-Jo had thought about becoming a priest, but he was much more taken with the starched sisters, who knew what was what and who was who. Jo-Jo was not at all like Father Petroni.

I WAS STARTING TO WANT A cigarette. I had a pack up at the cabin. "Can we go inside?"

"Sure," said Phoebe with a distracted air. She floated behind me as I labored up the steep path to the cabin. "You really ought to stop smoking. This walk isn't that steep."

"Not for you," I panted.

She sighed. "Guardian angels spend all their time protecting people from themselves."

"Seems to me you could have protected me more from my big sister."

"Nah. Big sisters are good for building character."

"Big sisters, bad boyfriends, and a lot of other things, apparently."

Phoebe didn't answer. She seemed to be thinking hard. We brushed past the meadow grasses, and I opened the cabin door. I slipped a cigarette out of the pack and lit it. I lay down on the worn Navajo rug in the middle of the floor and propped my feet up on the old wicker armchair in the corner.

"So what's Jo-Jo going to be when he grows up?"

"Aren't you going to write any of this down?"

"I'll remember it." I practiced blowing smoke rings. I had no intention of writing her story, but I figured Phoebe needed to get this out of her system. "Why do you want to write about someone like Jo-Jo?" I asked.

"I don't know," Phoebe shrugged. "He reminds me a little bit of an angel."

I watched my smoke rings drift toward the rough pine beams that crossed the ceiling. They disintegrated when they touched wood. "So this is a story about an angel?"

I sat up to light another cigarette. From outside the open window, I heard the sounds of grasshoppers and crickets. Through the scent of lighter fluid and burning tobacco, a warm breeze brought the smell of the sun on the meadow grasses. The breeze blew across the fine blonde hairs on my arm. Phoebe's nightgown didn't flutter at all, but I thought I saw her long hair move ever so slightly in the air of this world.

"I think it's more about you," Phoebe said. She floated up against the ceiling and disappeared.

I pondered the mystery of Jo-Jo and me and whether I had anything in common with a baby faggot who wanted to get himself to a nunnery. My immediate conclusion was that I did not. That settled, I raised myself off the floor and went into the bedroom, where I threw on a T-shirt and a pair of shorts over my bathing suit. I was modest even when I was by myself. I wandered into the tiny kitchen and opened the refrigerator door. I removed the top from a can of tuna and held it upside down over the sink to drain the water. I made my sandwich. I sat down on one of the bar stools that ringed the kitchen counter. Phoebe floated back down into sight through the ceiling.

"Jo-Jo is really an outsider," I said.

"That's an understatement," muttered Phoebe.

"I don't think I could stand to be on the outside like that."

"Couldn't you?" Her look at me was quizzical.

"I don't think I could be that brave."

"Ah," she said. "Maybe not."

Phoebe had been such a blabbermouth all afternoon that it bothered me now she was being oblique. "Say what you mean," I said. "I know what you're thinking."

"What am I thinking?" asked Phoebe.

"You're thinking I'm not brave."

"I didn't really say that."

"I don't see a problem with keeping my personal life separate from my work life."

"And what personal life would that be?"

"I get a lot of satisfaction from my job. I'm proud of how hard I work."

"That's nice."

"That's enough for me."

"Good."

"I'm not ashamed, if that's what you mean."

"There's nothing to be ashamed of, is there?"

"I'll love whom I please," I said.

"When have you loved anyone?"

I turned my back on Phoebe. I grabbed the spy thriller that I was halfway through and plopped down on the couch. I started reading where I had left off—in the middle of a detailed description of the boiler room of a Russian submarine. When I glanced up, I didn't see Phoebe anywhere.

I used to have my life perfectly arranged into two worlds. By day I had a good job as Alice the Manager in a computer software company. By night and weekend, I was Alice the Lesbian who swam in the comfortable river of a community of women. The division between my days and my nights was as thin as a spider's web and as strong as steel. It had to be. Being out of the closet on the job was just great if you worked at my company and never expected to do more than exactly what they hired you to do. They wouldn't fire you. They'd just forget to promote you. Not one manager was openly gay. The only people out of the closet were the ones working for those of us who weren't.

In my college days, all I had in mind was that I wanted to be an artist. I quickly got over it once I graduated and realized that no one was around to support me in the style to which I wanted to become accustomed. So instead I fell back on my other talent: typing. I got a job writing computer manuals. I worked my way up, going from a bad company to one that was a little better to one that was a little better. I was smart enough to give up the thing I loved for the thing I could do. And I never regretted that.

As a manager, I was in charge of a bunch of technical writers whose task it was to turn semi-verbal programmers into articulate human beings. The writers were the amateurs among software experts, the dilettantes among dedicated statisticians. I knew how hard their job was. I praised them in their performance reviews, mostly, and told them what they were doing was very, very important, that no one else could do it as well as they did. They all had the wrong education for paying jobs; they were lucky to be here, my medieval studies majors and Ph.D.'s in philosophy. They knew full well they'd be making half their salary if they'd managed to land a position in their chosen field. I admired them for the same reason I admired myself: we were adaptable. We saw which way the wind was blowing and we landed on our feet. My favorite thing about myself was that I was a survivor.

I knew enough about the programmers' secret language to be able to trace the elegant structures in their code. I could tease meaning from the descriptions they had written in garbled English. I could make ten impossible things happen before lunch, agree to deadlines no sane person would agree to, because I (we all) knew the schedule would slip and, even if it didn't, we were willing to stay there all night, night after night. I committed my writers to this, and, amazingly, they did it. I have learned that people will do anything if they believe they are needed. In fact, the harder their job is and the worse you treat them, the more enthusiastic they are.

None of my writers knew this, but I liked to get to work very early in the morning, before the cleaning people left. I stopped outside every door along the hallway to my office and thought about that person as though he or she were a subject in my kingdom. My office was the only one with a window; I could look out at the sun just topping the manicured trees and believe that everyone in the company was in harmony. I could believe that I was happy.

A change would come over me when I went home in the evenings. I would get very sleepy as I drove along the interstate, sleepy enough to be dangerous. As truck drivers barrelled past on their way to unload their cargo in time to get paid for the day, I would fall into a dreamlike state where I'd have to shake my head to stay in this world and out of the way of the semis. I'd be distracted by the tangled clouds around the setting sun. The sky would never be tamed, no matter how many blocks of identical houses and strip malls were laid out beneath it. The clouds swirled up toward heaven above the noisy highway.

By the time I turned into the parking lot in front of my condo, I'd be coming out of my post-work stupor and into my other life. Part of my ritual when I arrived home was to strip out of the linen suits and sensible pumps I wore on the job and slip into a pair of tattered jeans and a T-shirt. Then I went to the gym and sweated myself silly on the exercycle. After working out, I sat naked in the sauna with the other women and listened to the ones who were married complain about men. Sometimes the married women got a little flirty, which was amusing but made me nervous.

Friday evenings I went down to the Grill. Darlene's Grill occupied the second floor of the old Woolworth building downtown. Darlene was a big country girl who had a happy hour for women every Friday. I never knew who I'd see there: an ex-girlfriend I was terrified of running into while secretly wondering what she was doing these days and hoping she was miserable, women just passing through town, computer workers like me, attorneys, landscapers. We sat at long tables and consumed pitchers of beer or very sweet iced tea and we talked through the night. Happy hour could run into closing time.

I used to have a girlfriend named Beatrice who shared a house with two other women: a counselor of AIDS patients and a cook in a restaurant. There was also a poet who stayed with them now and then for a few weeks at a time.

Beatrice spent summers doing massage at women's festivals all over the country. She worked when she needed to and stopped working when she could. She learned a lot about people while she was massaging them. "It's like being a hairdresser," she said. "People tell you their secrets. Touching them brings out all the anguish they've been hiding."

I miss our talking. We talked together even in our sleep. I'd half wake up and hear myself babbling back to what she was saying in the middle of a dream. We spent weekends at her house. She never liked staying at my condo, even though it was much nicer than her place. I left a change of clothes in her room. I tried to always come back to my own bed on Sunday evenings, just to get myself in the right mindset for work. I didn't see her during the week. There wasn't enough time. On weeknights we talked to each other on the phone before we went to bed. If the counselor or the cook didn't need to use the phone, we kept the receivers cradled next to our ears all night so we could hear each other breathing in our sleep. Fridays we would find each other again at the Grill.

Beatrice kept canaries in her bedroom. They started singing merrily at the first hint of morning light. To forestall this, she threw a towel over their cage as we were undressing. We made love to muffled peeps as the canaries settled themselves in for the night.

I was awakened by the sound of a gunshot one morning. "Shit!" we shouted together. I sat up in bed. Beatrice was standing in the corner of the room in her T-shirt and boxers, a pistol in her hand. "Missed him!" she said.

"Missed who?"

"Cockroach. I hate those things."

There was a tiny, perfectly symmetrical hole in the wall across from the gun. I noticed a few more in the baseboard. The canaries fluttered and squawked beneath their towel.

"Jesus Christ," I said as I flopped back down on my pillow. "Next time try a shoe."

"Messes up the shoe," she said.

That was what life was like at Beatrice's house: you never knew what was going to happen next. The poet passed through on her spiritual journey and somehow the three of us ended up in a hot tub in a downtown hotel blowing soap bubbles that rose in the air above the churning waters.

My lesbian life had a certain Brigadoon-like quality, a fantasy world that was really nice to visit, but impossible to live in. There were some, though, like Beatrice, who stayed in the paradise of the downwardly mobile, among women who spent their whole lives choosing to work at minimum wage for political causes, or traveling around the country selling crafts at women's festivals. On Monday mornings, I came down out of Brigadoon and into the real world.

Beatrice sent a dozen roses to my office on our first Valentine's Day. I had just gotten out of a meeting with the vice president; I was in line for a promotion. When the receptionist called me, I knew she had read the card that was attached to them because she told me who they were from. I scooped them off her desk, rushed them out to the parking lot, and shoved them into the trunk of my car. That damned receptionist probably gossiped about it to all the other secretaries over lunch.

It was a really cold Valentine's Day. The roses froze in the trunk; they'd turned black by the time I arrived home, and I tossed them in the dumpster on my way in. Beatrice couldn't afford what she had done. She was waiting in my condo, happy, expecting me to bring the roses home and love her for sending them, and I was angry with her for trying to out me, for making me feel guilty, for crossing the boundary I had set up so carefully between work and life.

"So what'd you think?" She had lit candles all over my apartment. There was no other light but the little flames that shone in every room. I didn't answer at first, I was so angry. I stalked into my bedroom, swept off my coat, and practically knocked over the candlestick that was flickering on my dresser. I hung up my coat, took a deep breath, and walked slowly back into the living room where she was waiting still.

"What the fuck were you doing?" I hissed. "Are you trying to destroy me? Is that what you want? So I have to live like you and take any shitty job I can find, just like you?"

Her face was frozen in shock. People's faces really do freeze. It's not like the movies, where their eyes bug out or their mouths fall open. That's acting. When they're really shocked, they're frozen in time, as though if they hold onto the same expression, time will go backward and the thing that frightened them will disappear. I was panting I was so angry.

"I'm sorry," I finally said. I wasn't. Yet. "But don't ever do that to me again."

"Where are they?" That was all she could manage to say.

"In the dump."

She closed her eyes. Then she opened them and swiped at them with the sleeve of her shirt. I was the only one fighting that evening. That's what survivors have to do.

"I'll be going," she said. She pulled on her coat and dabbed at her eyes again. She closed the door quietly behind her.

I turned on the lights and blew out the candles, one by one. The air stunk of burned wax. She should have asked first. She should have sent them to my condo. Or sent no flowers at all since she couldn't afford them. On the dining room table was a small gift-wrapped box. I sat down and stared at it. Damn her. Inside the box was a tiny framed picture of us together, the fall before, in the mountains.

I never set out the picture she gave me. I kept it in my underwear drawer, at the back, with the sachets that had lost all their scent. I suppose it's still there.

I didn't see Phoebe for months after she appeared to me in the mountains. At five o'clock one April morning, I was finishing up the second chapter in a manual that still had four chapters to go and a deadline in three days. Dimly, outside my window, I could discern the chirps of birds waking up in the false dawn. We couldn't open our windows, of course. We could watch nature, but not touch it through the glass. I stretched until I could hear my joints pop. I went outside to hear the birds more clearly and to smoke a cigarette. A mockingbird sang a swooping aria from a cherry tree next to my office building. If I looked to the east, I could imagine a little bit of light there. I stubbed out my cigarette and breathed in deeply before turning to go back inside. Out of the corner of my eye, I caught a flicker of something white. Another bird, I guessed, probably a pigeon. I headed toward the glass doors. Something else shimmered just past the boundary of my peripheral vision. I quickly turned my head and saw nothing. Sleeplessness will do that to you, make the air move and the sidewalks shift.

I was alone on my end of the building this early morning; the last of my writers had gone home several hours ago. I poured myself another cup of coffee and padded back down the empty hallway to my office. I kept hearing a sound like feathers, or whispers. I settled back into my chair to type. The whispering blended in with the white noise from the heating vents.

I heard the first writer come in for the day. Mary, who was writing a book about operating systems, stuck her head in my door and said, "Been here all night?" I nodded and she shook her head. Mary went away. There was someone sitting in the chair in the corner of my office. I hadn't noticed them come in. I turned to speak to whoever it was and caught a glimpse of red before it became obvious that there was no one sitting in the chair at all.

Later that afternoon, Mary came into my office again and sat down on the overstuffed armchair I kept in the corner to make my visitors comfortable. My door was always open for my writers. I tried to meet with each of them every two weeks. Sometimes we had a glass of sherry, especially if our meeting was at the end of the day. They visited my office, one by one, and sat with me in the sunlight. It was the only chance they got to see the sun. Mary and I often talked about mythology and religion. She had been a Classics major, with a minor in Fine Arts. She made a clay pot for me every Christmas. I smiled at her and closed the monthly report I was writing up.

She settled down into the corner armchair.

"Sherry?" I asked.

She shook her head. She looked tired. I knew she'd been working a lot of overtime. She said, "What would you be doing if you didn't have to earn a living?"

"You mean if I won the lottery?"

"Whatever. What would you do?"

I didn't tell her about Phoebe's plans for my life. "I don't know. Sleep in, I guess. Travel. Make a few investments."

"I'd be a potter," Mary said dreamily. The stress was getting to her. She sighed and stared into space. "I'd make pots. Just pots for people to cook or grow flowers in. Clay. No words."

In the dust that floated in the sunlight I caught a glimpse of something white and fluttering and Phoebe-like. "Not now, Phoebe,"

I thought. I tensed my forehead and closed my mind.

Mary said, "Maybe I will have that sherry."

I hoped she was almost done with her manual. It didn't seem like the right time to ask if she could meet her deadline. I poured from the bottle I kept in my filing cabinet into a plastic cup and handed it to her. She held the cheap golden sherry up to the sun and turned the cup in her hand.

"Don't you miss college?" she asked. "Don't you miss thinking about God and philosophy and art? Didn't you ever believe that Art was your real calling?"

I could now see Phoebe clearly, floating just behind Mary's head. I said, "Nope. Never. Don't you think you'd get bored, making pots day after day after day?"

"My studio would be full of light. I'd listen to opera while I centered the pots on the wheel. Each day I'd form shapes no one had ever seen before."

Eventually Mary wandered away, leaving me with my sherry and the setting sun. That night I lay awake and pictured her in her bright studio, throwing centered shapes. I thought about the time when I was going to be an artist someday, and how I was such a different person then. I tried to push the feeling of loss away from me. That happy girl so caught up in her own creations had nothing to do with who I was now. Phoebe appeared against the ceiling. She glowed in the dark.

"You."

"I like Mary," said Phoebe.

I turned over and put my face in my pillow. I could feel Phoebe's breath on my neck. I pretended to be asleep.

"Wake up," she said. "I've got another idea for a story. It's called 'Don't Give Up Your Day Job.'"

I snored lightly. After a while, I no longer felt Phoebe's presence in the room.

During a meeting on marketing strategies the next day, I doodled in the margin of my notes while the head of the company droned on about "targeting" and "selling 'til it hurts."

I have to be careful now that I'm in management that my doodles won't be misinterpreted by unfriendly eyes, so I make rebuses, little sequences of pictures that spell out what I'm really thinking. To make TEDIOUS, I had drawn a teapot for TEA, a musical bar with a D note, and two round people that were meant to be me and Phoebe (identifiable by her wings) for US. It was sort of a private game of charades. I started to write something else in the margin. I looked at my hand curiously: BAD GIRL GOES TO HELL, BEATS HELL OUT OF DEVIL.

Phoebe again. "Doesn't that sound like a fun story?" she whispered. I put my hand over my ear and stared at the CEO as though I were paying attention. Maybe it was because I was tired and my resistance was down, but I couldn't picture anything but the Bad Girl in my mind. I wondered what her story was.

After the meeting, I walked over to the company cafeteria for lunch. I brought my plate outside and sat down under an oak tree to watch the stream of workers flowing down the sidewalk below me.

"The Bad Girl is blonde," I said.

"Yes," said Phoebe. "A brassy blonde. And she's a little top-heavy. She wears her sweaters too tight."

"She sounds kind of fifties."

"She reminds me of Patsy Cline," said Phoebe.

"Tough, and vulnerable."

"Heart of gold."

A grackle chuckled in the branches above my head.

"Her name is Blanche," I said. "She's smart. Uneducated, but smart."

"Where does she live?" asked Phoebe.

"She lives in eastern North Carolina. She works at the hosiery mill. She likes to fish. She's had all her teeth pulled, and she has a full set of very white new ones. She has a skinny little bandy-legged husband named Ervin. They got married the day after they graduated from high school. There were only ten students in their senior class. Whenever anybody asks Blanche why she married so young, she shrugs and says, 'Nothing else to do.' The nearest movie theater is twenty miles away."

Phoebe floated up to sit on the branch next to the grackle, which didn't seem to be bothered by her presence. She said, "Blanche and

Ervin live in a trailer park where the grass has been beaten down into the sandy soil. They have three pale blond kids. Two boys and a girl. At the time of this story, there's also a beagle puppy that doesn't stop barking until somebody pays attention to him."

"Blanche is thirty-eight," I said. "She has beautiful handwriting, which she uses when she signs her checks and when she sends postcards to her cousins back home from the family's annual trip to Myrtle Beach."

"Carolina Beach," said Phoebe. "Myrtle Beach would be too expensive."

"Right. Their trailer has rust spots on the outside. The two boys share a tiny bedroom, and the girl has another smaller one. Blanche and Ervin sleep in the master bedroom at the end of the hall. The inside of the trailer smells of too many people living together too closely. Blanche feels like a giant in her own home. The children are small and wiry, like their father. They were designed to live in a trailer, but Blanche's body is meant for bigger spaces."

"Do Blanche and Ervin love each other?" asked Phoebe.

"They think of each other as the hand they were dealt. Ervin never touches hard liquor, but he drinks beer constantly, at the body shop where he sprays paint over old cars to make them new again, out back of the trailer where he barbecues on Saturday afternoons, when he and Blanche fish in the creek that runs by the side of the trailer park."

Phoebe fluttered down onto the grass next to me. She plucked a blade of grass and put it in her mouth.

"Does Blanche drink?" she asked.

"Not as much as Ervin. One of them needs to be sober at home, for the children's sake. She lets herself loose on Friday nights when she and her girlfriends from the mill go to the motel lounge on the outskirts of town. They sit at a big round table in the corner of the lounge and tell dirty stories about their husbands or the men at work."

"Blanche doesn't like hard liquor, either," said Phoebe.

"She drinks Paul Masson rosé. It gives her a headache all the next day."

"So Blanche and her girlfriends are sitting around this table in a corner of the motel lounge one night...," said Phoebe.

"...And Blanche's best friend Donna says, 'I heard Shaquita and Bernard were doing it,'" I continued.

"'No!' says Blanche. 'Are you shitting me? Does his wife know about that?' Bernard is white and Shaquita is black.

"'She might be relieved to have somebody else lie down for that old goat,' says Donna. Bernard's gut hangs over his belt. He repairs the machinery at the mill. When he crouches down to tighten a bolt near the floor, the crack in his pale white butt shows above his pants.

"'Poor Shaquita,' says Blanche. 'If she had to do it with a white man, she could've picked somebody better than Bernard.'"

Phoebe lay down on the grass and folded her hands behind her head. The sidewalk had emptied. It was time to go back to the office.

"What's sex like?" she asked.

"It's hard to describe to someone who doesn't have a body."

"Is it ecstasy?"

"Sometimes. Sometimes it's boring. Sometimes it's painful. Sometimes it's too close. Sometimes it's scary. It's complicated. Sometimes it's like the smell of coffee: the anticipation is much more exciting than the reality."

"I wouldn't know," said Phoebe.

"It's your turn," I said.

"After the conversation in the motel lounge," said Phoebe, "Blanche drives home very carefully. She's overdone the Paul Masson. Ervin is still up, untangling fishing line on the kitchen table. 'How you, honey,' Blanche calls when she comes into the kitchen. When Blanche has had too much to drink, she talks fast, as though she must hurry up and say what she needs to say so she can move on to the next thing she has to say.

"Ervin doesn't look up. He squints at the almost invisible line in his hands and says, 'Have a good time?'"

I picked up the thread of the story. "'Yeah. Unh-hunh,' Blanche calls over her shoulder as she goes down the narrow hallway to the master bedroom at the end. 'Kids in bed?'

"'Yup,' says Ervin. 'Tommy wanted to wait up for you, but I told him it'd be better if he saw you in the morning. They had dinner.'

"'What'd you give 'em? Fish sticks again?'

"'Nothin' wrong with fish sticks. I didn't give 'em no greens. I can't stand the fussin'.'" Ervin's sole culinary technique is to fry everything in a cup of oil.

"Blanche takes off her foundation garments and slips on her old nightgown and her long red bathrobe. She pads back up the hall to where Ervin sits at the kitchen table. She settles down heavily onto one of the grey vinyl kitchen chairs. She watches Ervin look cross-eyed at the fishing line. 'Any beer left?' she asks."

Phoebe stared up at the sky and turned the blade of grass around in her mouth. I wondered how she could do that when she couldn't touch anything. She tossed the grass onto the ground and folded her arms behind her head. I glanced furtively at the discarded blade. There were definitely teeth marks on it. She continued with our story.

"Ervin says, 'New case out on the back porch.' Blanche knows Ervin drinks too much, but at times like this it's convenient; they're never out of beer. 'You sure that's going to sit all right on top of the wine, hon?' Ervin asks the air as Blanche comes in from their back porch with a can for each.

"Blanche says, 'I'll just have the one to settle me down for the night.' Blanche can't stop herself from thinking about Shaquita and Bernard. When she pictures whites and blacks together, she sees a smartass teenage black boy with a silly white girl on his arm. She doesn't believe it's fair to the children to be neither race. When she stares at a couple like that walking around downtown in broad daylight, the black boy stares back at her, as though daring her to say something. Blanche never does say anything, but she keeps on looking right at them for all she's worth.

"But Blanche likes Shaquita. She's a nice quiet girl with a head on her shoulders. They work next to each other at the mill. They take their breaks together. Shaquita doesn't say too much. Blanche knows Shaquita is pretty young—she might still be in her teens. She lives down the highway on the other side of the river, in a place the whites call Niggertown and the blacks call Georgetown. Every morning at ten o'clock, Blanche and Shaquita and a few of the other girls go out to a picnic table in the yard behind the mill and smoke cigarettes. The breaks are the only time blacks and whites sit together. They go to different places for lunch.

"Sitting at the table with Ervin, sipping from the can of beer, Blanche is surprised at how little she knows about Shaquita now that she considers it. Blanche realizes maybe she doesn't even know whether Shaquita has any brothers and sisters. Maybe she just thinks she does because blacks have a lot of children."

I really should have been back at work by now but I didn't want to leave Blanche and Shaquita. Whoever walked by my empty office would assume I was in a meeting.

I said, "Ervin glances up at Blanche from his knotted line. 'Somethin' wrong?'

"'Do you know Bernard Nichols?'

"'That fat guy works at the mill?'

"'Yeah. Him.'

"'He comes around the shop sometimes. He's friends with Jimmy.' Jimmy and Ervin work together.

"'You like him?'

"'Can't say as I do or I don't. He talks too much.'

"Bernard gives Blanche the creeps. He stares at her titties like he wants to take a bite out of them. Ervin lights another cigarette and pulls more tangled line up from the floor next to his chair.

"'What the hell happened to your line?'

"'Reel broke.' The nylon line lies tangled in a cloud next to Ervin's elbow.

"'I'll say.' Blanche lights a Salem from Ervin's pack.

"'Help yourself, why don't you,' says Ervin. Blanche ignores him and puffs the menthol smoke across the table over his head. He's wearing a greasy grey ball cap tilted slightly back. The refrigerator motor kicks on with a loud throbbing hum.

"'Refrigerator's about to go,' says Blanche.

"'Hope it waits until I get a raise.'

"'You and me both,' says Blanche.

"'How come you wanted to know about Bernard?'

"Blanche considers whether or not to tell Ervin about Bernard and Shaquita. Maybe it's already a big joke around the shop, all those old boys talking about Shaquita.

"'You know Bernard's wife?' asks Blanche.

"'Didn't know he was still married.'

"'Do you know if he's got a girlfriend?'

"'Nope. Why? You interested?'

"'Shut up.'

"Ervin looks up for a minute from his tangled fishing line and meets Blanche's eyes. He goes back to his line."

I paused. "I like Blanche," I said. "I didn't think I was going to, but I do."

"Yeah, she's a good old girl," said Phoebe.

The manicured lawns of the office park were very quiet. The doors to the glass buildings that stood in a rectangle around the grass were closed. For the moment, I could not imagine what went on inside those walls.

"I really need to finish my monthly report." I said this without conviction.

Phoebe said, "Can't you wait until we know what happens next with Blanche? You can work late this evening."

"Let's go for a walk."

"Good idea."

I walked toward the company lake. I could feel Phoebe hovering behind me, for once in the spot that guardian angels were supposed to occupy.

"Blanche, Blanche, Blanche," I said. A programmer passing me on the sidewalk looked at me curiously. "Oops," I said, after she was out of earshot. "Perhaps we ought to go somewhere more secluded."

Without a second thought, I went to the parking lot and my car. I would not be missed for just one afternoon. I drove home to my condo, where the afternoon sun streamed down on the wall-to-wall carpeting. I was never there at this time of day. The complex was quiet. I was seeing a secret world that was hidden from those of us who had to work. I made myself a cup of tea and settled down on the couch. Phoebe sat on a chair next to the kitchen table. I noticed that she wasn't floating.

"A ngels are nothing, you know." Phoebe leaned on the table and stared glumly out the window. A woman lugged shopping bags up the stairs that led into the building across the parking lot from mine. "We don't have vices or virtues. We are nothing but invisible mirrors, reflecting back the light of God."

I thought she had personality to spare, some of it annoying enough to be considered sinful. "You have feelings, right?"

"Right," she sighed. "We can talk a good game. We just can't be in it."

"How would you go about being human?" I scratched an itch above my left knee. Phoebe had probably never had an itch.

"Being in a body that felt things would be fun. There seems to be more to it than that, though. I'd need to be able to sin."

"That's not *all* we do."

"Sin and do good works."

I thought a minute. "I don't know what sin is anymore."

"What's wrong with the old standards?"

"Like...?"

Phoebe ticked them off on her translucent fingers: "pride, covetousness, lust, anger, gluttony, envy, sloth."

I shook my head. "Hell, you need those just to get through the day."

"And what about the seven virtues?"

I had even less of an idea what those were. Probably not as useful as the first list.

Phoebe recited: "Wisdom, courage, temperance, justice, faith, hope, charity."

"Charity is the same as love, right?" I asked.

"Pretty much," she said.

"But not the same as lust?"

"Lust is love with a twist." Phoebe drummed her fingers on the windowsill. "It's hard to sin without a body."

"You could practice all the virtues without one," I said.

The clock ticked on the kitchen wall. "What's it like to know you're going to die?" she asked.

"Gee, thanks, Phoebe."

"I'm serious. What's it like?"

"I try not to think about it."

"How does it make you feel?"

"Like I said, I don't think about it."

"You said you try not to think about it."

I rooted through my pockets to find a pack of cigarettes. I pulled out a bent one, straightened it with my fingers, and lit it. "It scares me, okay? I don't want to die. I don't think I should have to. I really don't get your complaining. You don't feel pain, you don't die, you never have to worry about the clock running out."

"I wish I knew what time was," she sighed.

"It's 4:30." Phoebe didn't find that amusing. I sat my cup of tea down on the coffee table in front of the couch. "When Blanche goes to work at the mill on Monday," I said, "she glances over at Shaquita, who's working at the loom next to hers. Shaquita doesn't look as though she's keeping a secret. At break time, they walk outside together.

"The women around the table talk about their weekends. Donna and her family went all the way over to Charlotte to Carowinds. 'You shoulda seen me on the waterslide,' she says. 'I flew down that thing like a greased pig.' The women laugh and shake their heads.

"'You have a good weekend, Shaquita?' Blanche says to her. The women stop talking.

"'It was nice,' says Shaquita. She smiles shyly and looks down at the ground. 'Some choirs came in from out of town and sang at our church.'

"'I bet they sounded real pretty,' says Blanche. She's sorry she asked Shaquita that question in front of everybody else. The whole mill must have heard the rumor, judging from how the women got quiet to hear what Shaquita had to say. On the far side of the lawn, Blanche sees Bernard standing with the other men. He spits a wad of tobacco onto the grass. He looks over at where the women are sitting.

"That afternoon, Blanche is standing at her loom when she notices that Shaquita is gone. Blanche glances up at the big clock; she must have slipped out early. She doesn't see Bernard's ugly self around either."

"It's funny," interrupted Phoebe. "It's funny how stories get to a place where the path forks and you don't know which one to take. Like right now. I'm wondering if Blanche should take up with a black man, if she should beat Bernard up, or if she'll turn against both Shaquita and Bernard."

I said, "If we keep the title, I don't think she'll turn against Shaquita. The 'Devil' is probably Blanche's fear. Or Bernard. Hey, is there really a devil, Phoebe?" Phoebe's presence implied the existence of a whole host of spiritual beings, not all of whom I was sure I wanted to meet personally.

"We can be as good as or as bad as you can imagine."

I wasn't sure who "we" was. Angels? Human beings? Both? The concept of Phoebe as a devil in disguise was not comforting. "We who?" I asked.

"Human beings."

"Why'd you say 'we'?"

"Slip of the tongue, I guess." She walked into the kitchen. "Got anything to eat in here?"

"There's a bag of potato chips in the cupboard."

"I see it."

I heard a crackling. Phoebe came out of the kitchen clutching the half-empty bag. She had put a potato chip into her mouth, but she didn't seem to know quite what to do with it after that.

"What in the world are you doing?"

The bag slipped out of Phoebe's hand onto the floor. She tried to chew the potato chip. She looked down at the bag at her feet as though it were a snake and she had no idea how it had gotten there.

"Yikes," she said with her mouth full. "How did that happen?"

"You're eating. And carrying things around."

"I'm not supposed to be able to do that."

"That's what you told me."

She glided just above the floor over to where I was sitting on the couch. "Touch me," she said.

I put my hand on her arm. It was smooth and cool. Her arm was translucent—I could just see her nightgown shimmering behind it, but she was solid to the touch.

"Can you feel my hand?" I asked.

"I had no idea mortals had such hot skin. Why do you even bother to wear clothes?"

"To keep our heat from escaping."

"This is fun." Phoebe floated around my living room, touching everything. She was surprised by the spines on the cactus. She peered at her finger.

"You're not bleeding, are you?"

"No." She held her translucent finger up to the light coming in from the window. "Didn't make a mark. Is that pain?"

"Of a sort. Not a very big pain."

She floated into the kitchen. I smelled something odd, like hot glass. I heard a muffled squeak. I hurried to the kitchen door. Phoebe was examining her hand again. The burner on the electric stove was bright red.

"Are you all right?"

"So that's pain."

"I should say. Are you sure you're all right?"

"Yes. It hurt, though. Now that I know what 'hurt' is."

"Does it still hurt?"

"It stopped as soon as I took my hand away from the burner."

"Is your hand hot?"

She held it out to me. Her skin was as cool as before.

I said, "Stop doing that. It's making me hurt just watching you."

"Ah," she said. "'Referred pain.'"

"That usually means feeling pain in a different part of the same body," I said.

"That fits," said Phoebe.

As I walked back out of the kitchen, I felt something touching the back of my hair. I stood still as Phoebe's glass fingers explored every strand. She floated around to the front of my head and patted my face, delicately, like a butterfly walking. I shut my eyes, and felt the *dot-dot-dot* of the ends of her fingers on my eyelids. She stuck a finger into my ear.

"Oooooh," I shivered.

"Ears are sensitive," she said in the tone of someone making a mental note. She patted her hands down the front of my blouse, over my hips, down my legs. She was particularly intrigued by my suede pumps. She rubbed the nap in different directions. When she was done with my shoes, she staggered away, a drunk angel. She touched the dining room table, the walls, the carpet, the glass of the window, which made her pause for a moment, around and around the apartment, faster and faster, until she collapsed in a corner of the room, a glazed expression on her face.

"How do you stand it?" she asked. "Feeling all the time is exhausting." She lifted one hand weakly and patted the side of the couch, since it was there. "Ugh. I don't want to touch anything." She rose from the carpet an inch or two so she wouldn't have to be in contact with it.

"What are we going to do about Blanche?" I asked.

"Oh. Blanche. Hell if I know." I hoped she didn't mean that literally. Her answer about the devil had been rather vague. "I need a nap," she said.

"Can you sleep?"

"I'll just close my eyes for a second." She shut her eyes as she floated above the carpet. She was still sitting up. Her head dropped to one side and I heard a faint snore. The sunlight streaming through the windows had turned more golden as the afternoon deepened. I heard the cries of children squabbling out front. I made myself a second cup of tea and settled back down on the couch. I wondered what "Don't Give Up Your Day Job" was about.

"D on't Give Up Your Day Job" must be about an artist, I thought, somebody who had to go to work every day, away from her first love. I liked the color of the light that shone from the sky into my room. I would make "Don't Give Up Your Day Job" be about a painter. She was wearing a man's shirt that had been white before it became spattered with blotches of paint. Her studio was in a warehouse downtown that had been converted into drafty apartments with high ceilings. The windows reached from floor to ceiling. Across from the warehouse was an automobile body shop and an abandoned electrical parts distributor. Carla (seemed like a good name) liked Sundays in winter the best, when the clear light shone on the empty street below the window. She felt as though she lived in an Edward Hopper painting then.

I decided that Carla wasn't a painter; instead she built little boxes that held complicated scenes. She used junk mail, plastic figurines from the toy store, rubbish she found on the street to build her rectangular worlds. Stacked against one wall of her studio were rows of these boxes. They had scenic backdrops cut from magazines—

oceans, forests, sharp cliffs against which her plastic cowboys and Indians clung.

She tended bar at night in a restaurant where theater people hung out. She stood over six feet tall. She had flaming red hair that cascaded to her waist. Her face was beautiful: high cheekbones, high coloring.

I tiptoed past Phoebe to my bedroom. I sat down at my desk and pulled a pen out of the mason jar I kept there. On the legal pad that I had arranged at a precise ninety-degree angle from the edge, I started to write.

BEFORE SHE FALLS ASLEEP in the small hours of the morning, Carla lies on her king-sized futon on the floor of her studio lit by the streetlight. Rectangular boxes containing scenes with tiny plastic people and animals are stacked on the wall next to the bed. Each box is separate from the other; each world is aware only of itself. It's like the wall of TVs at Circuit City: each screen is broadcast by a different station. Timmy looks for Lassie, Vanna moves her letters, Jim wrestles with a giant anaconda.

In the sunlit day before night falls and she has to go to work, Carla sits at the kitchen table and leans her enormous form over the tiny figures in a box. Her big hands delicately apply the glue and sequins, and position the swatches of greenery that represent trees. Her red hair flames over the back of the chair behind her.

Sometimes she sells a box to someone who has heard of them, and her, and stops by the studio. Two boxes sit behind the bar at the restaurant where she tends bar. She is interested in what the patrons say about what the boxes mean. Their meaning is never what she intended.

"WHO'S CARLA?"

I jumped. I hadn't heard Phoebe float into the room. "She's who 'Don't Give Up Your Day Job' is about."

Phoebe hovered just behind me, reading over my shoulder. I hated that. She nodded. "Sounds interesting," she said, "but what do the scenes inside the boxes look like?"

I chewed on the end of my pen. The ends of all my pens looked like they'd been through a meat grinder. "They're scenes from Carla's life."

I turned to a clean page on the legal pad and drew a rectangle in the middle. Inside the rectangle I drew a stick figure lying down. Around the stick figure I drew other stick figures, standing. "Their backs are turned to the one that's lying down," I said. In the sky I drew a smiling sun and puffy clouds. Then I drew a dog next to the horizontal stick figure.

"This is Carla's father." I touched the stick figure that was lying down with the point of my pen. "And these," I waved my pen over the other figures, "are the rest of Carla's family, and a neighbor."

"Is Carla there?" asked Phoebe.

"No. She's over here." I drew a house in the corner of the rectangle, with a round head in one of the upstairs windows. "Carla's father was an alcoholic, but no one in the family talked about it. One Saturday morning, when Carla was eleven years old, she looked out the window of her bedroom and saw her father lying in the driveway. He stroked his arms across the gravel as though he were swimming. He smiled helplessly. Through the closed bedroom window, Carla saw his mouth form words she couldn't hear.

"Carla's mother was chatting with a neighbor. Her mother and the neighbor kept on with their conversation as though there were no man on the ground next to them. Carla's dog, Flannery, sniffed curiously at her father's head, and then ambled off to investigate something more interesting. No one mentioned the incident afterwards. Carla has put it into a box to make it real."

"What do other people think of this box?" Phoebe asked.

"They think the plastic figures are dancing, and that the one lying down in the middle is part of the dance. Carla put a mirror in the back so they could see themselves in the scene."

"So every box is a story," said Phoebe.

"Sometimes it's just one chapter."

Phoebe floated to the middle of the bedroom. She seemed to be avoiding physical contact with anything.

"Are all the boxes about Carla?"

"Lately," I said, "Carla has started to branch out into the lives of her friends, or the lives she reads about in the newspaper." I drew another rectangle on the paper. I drew a winged figure inside the rectangle.

"What are you doing? Stop that!" Phoebe was at my shoulder again.

"All's fair in art and war," I said. "I can draw you if I want to." I drew a round smiley face on the winged figure.

"Yuck," said Phoebe.

I drew a balloon coming out from the smiley face's mouth. Inside the balloon I printed HAVE A NICE DAY.

Phoebe tried to grab the pen out of my hand, but she couldn't get a grip on it.

I covered the paper with rectangles stacked atop each other, until it was a solid grid of vertical and horizontal lines. The rectangles were blank, ready to be filled. I started shading them in, one by one, carefully, as though this were an important task. My mind was as empty as one of the rectangles.

"I see Carla in two places," said Phoebe. "The bar and her studio. I see Carla and her boxes in those places. I don't see Carla without her boxes."

"I do," I said. "I see her striding down the winter street toward the warehouse. She wears a wool cape slung over her broad shoulders. In boots she's about six-foot four. She moves likes a monument through the streets of the city."

"Carla doesn't talk much," said Phoebe.

"No," I said. "Her mother used to say, 'Carla is my pensive one.'" Carla goes to parties with other artists. She stands in the background, watching. Sometimes she puts a party into a box."

Phoebe said, "That's what Carla was doing in the box she made of herself and her father: watching. Does she have a lover?"

"Her size intimidates people and keeps them at a distance. She is usually glad about this."

"What about friends?"

"She has friends," I said, a bit defensively. Carla was starting to sound like a mass murderer, one of the quiet ones you ought to keep an eye on. Phoebe raised an eyebrow. "Okay, okay," I said. "Let's see.

The other bartender at the restaurant...he's the one who suggested she put her boxes on display there. Her best friend, Angelica, who is tiny and paints enormous abstracts. Carla has lots of friends."

"No lovers, though," said Phoebe. Why was Phoebe making Carla look like a loser?

"Not yet."

"Can she have one?"

"Is that what you want this story to be about?"

"I want to know more about this sex business," said Phoebe. "You didn't really give me an answer when I asked you what it was like, and it doesn't look like Blanche is going to get any any time soon."

"Don't be crude, Phoebe."

"That's what you're supposed to say, isn't it? *Get some. Get any. Have you had any lately?*"

I had a trash-talking guardian angel. "Angelica has a brother named Frederico, who is as small as a jockey," I said. Phoebe folded her hands behind her head and leaned back in the air above the bed so she could listen more comfortably. She smiled. "Oh, boy," she said.

I shot her a disgusted look. "Anyway," I said, "Frederico reminds Carla of one of her plastic figures. He wears pointed black cowboy boots with silver toes. The hard heels of his boots *click-click-click* when he walks down the sidewalk. Frederico moves like the dancer he is. Even drunk, he stumbles like Fred Astaire.

"He often visits Carla's studio with his sister. Carla knows who's coming to visit her by the *click-click-click* of Frederico's heels on the metal staircase, accompanied by the soft thud of Angelica's shoes. Frederico and Angelica run up the two flights of stairs. When they go walking together, Carla is in the middle. Each of her long strides is equal to three of Frederico's and Angelica's precise steps.

"One Saturday afternoon, Carla is putting the finishing touches on a box about a bicycle trip she took by herself to the coast. Against the backdrop she pastes a magazine photograph of the ocean. *Carmen* blasts from the CD player, filling the apartment with Jessye Norman, another monumental woman whom Carla admires. 'L'amour, l'amour...' sings Jessye. Carla loves this solo. She stands up and lip syncs with Jessye. She spreads her arms out to embrace her apartment, the sun outside, all the world. Tears spring to her eyes, she loves the song so much. She twirls across the floor, a colossal figure turned by flight into an archangel. The song ends, and she moves to the CD player to cue the song up again.

"On her way across the room she hears *click-click-click* on the metal stairs. She listens for the soft thud of Angelica's steps next to the clicks. The clicks stop outside her door. There is a soft *rap-rap*, a pause, then a second *rap-rap*.

"When she opens the door, Frederico holds out a paper bag. Carla takes the bag and says, 'Come in.' He smiles when he walks inside.

"'I like this place,' he says. 'It is as big as you are.'

"Carla blushes. She is proud of her size. 'Thanks, Freddie.'

"'Look in the bag to see what I've brought you.'

"Carla sets the gift next to the box she's been working on. Frederico sits on the stool on the other side of the table and entwines his legs through its wooden limbs. Carla opens the bag and peers inside. She thinks she sees tiny arms and legs, all in a tangle. She holds the bag upside down. Out tumble plastic people in many colors—purple and red and yellow and green. There are animals too—monkeys and whales and tortoises and snakes and horses.

"'Wow!' Carla says. She holds up two handfuls of the little plastic figures and lets them tumble down between her fingers as though they were gold.

"'My cousin's kids are all grown. She was about to throw these beauties out. Can you believe it?'

"Carla sorts through the pile of figures in front of her and extricates the human ones. She lines them up in a tiny parade along the edge of the table: marching bow-legged cowboys separated from their horses, warriors with sword arms outstretched, mostly missing their swords, Greek goddesses dashing forward. The line goes from one end of Carla's work table to the other and halfway back again.

"'Look at this one.' She sets down the last figure bringing up the rear of the parade. 'This must be you.' It's a tapdancer, on his toes, arms spread out to the side. His plastic base is broken, and he won't stay upright. She leans him against the side of the box.

"Frederico peers at the dancer's face. 'His nose is chewed off.'

"'Your cousin's kids must've liked this one the best.'

"'I think the dog is really responsible for his condition.' He points at a goddess. 'This one is you. See what long strides she takes.' The red statue looks as though she's bounding over mountains. Her plastic hair sticks out behind her head. She's wearing a short toga. Her feet are bare.

"The animals lie in a pile, their limbs entangled. Carla pulls them over to her and starts to sort them out. There's a third pile of trees and fences and houses that Frederico starts to work on."

"Hurry up," said Phoebe.

"Hurry up what?"

"Get to the sex scene."

"Sex is ninety percent anticipation." It was growing dark outside. I couldn't hear the squabbling children in the parking lot anymore. Lights from cars turning into the apartment complex on their way home to families and dinner flashed against the window and then were gone. We sat in the dark, on opposite sides of the room. She glowed faintly, just enough for me to make out the shape of her wings and her hair.

"Carla," I said, "has a box of tiny jars of paint, with little brushes. When she and Frederico have sorted the figures into people, animals, and scenery, she picks up a blue man and begins to delicately apply brown paint to his face.

"'Who is that?' asks Frederico.

"'His name is Jo-Jo,' Carla says. She sets him on the end of the table to dry."

"Wait a minute," said Phoebe. "Jo-Jo?"

"You remember Jo-Jo."

"Jo-Jo of the snow?"

"Yep."

"Huh," mused Phoebe.

Carla places the box of her bicycle trip down on the floor next to the table. Frederico picks it up and looks inside.

"'I like this one,' he says. 'I like to think of you alone, with the wind and the sea. You are as strong as they are.'

"Carla thinks Frederico has gone a bit overboard.

"'May I have this one?' he asks her.

"Carla looks at him in surprise. The boxes are hers. She doesn't even like to sell them. The one time she gave a show at a local gallery she put SOLD stickers on all the boxes so no one would buy them. She wishes she still had the few that she has sold. She dreams of sneaking into the houses of their owners in the middle of the night and stealing back her creations.

"'Can't you just look at it when you visit?' she asks.

"Frederico sighs. 'Okay. I will do that.' He lays his hands gently, palms down, on the top of the box. 'I want to live with this scene and see it every day.'

"Frederico has curly black hairs on his wrists and the backs of his hands. Beneath the black hairs, his skin is very pale. Carla puts her big tanned hand atop his, which are still on the box. Against her palm she feels his knuckles and the smooth edges of his fingernails. Frederico wiggles his fingers against Carla's palm and smiles at her. Carla suddenly feels nervous. 'What's Angelica up to this afternoon?'

"'I think she went shopping, maybe. I'm not sure.'

"'Would you like some tea?' Carla gets up from the work table.

"'Yes. Very much.'

"Carla makes tea at the little stove in the corner of her apartment that is her kitchen. She doesn't look at Frederico. She can feel him watching her. She feels too big and clumsy. She pours the boiling water into two cups and swaps a tea bag between them. 'Sugar? Milk?' she calls, too loudly.

"'I'll get them.' Frederico jumps up from his stool and walks behind Carla to the refrigerator, his boot heels clicking against the bare wood floor. The slight breeze of his passing smells of patchouli. The two of them carry the makings of their tea to the work table. They push the piles of figures aside to clear a space."

It had grown too dark in my apartment to make out the rectangles on the legal pad. I imagined that each one held a different scene.

"Is the ninety percent up yet?" asked Phoebe.

"We'll see," I said.

"It's amazing you people manage to reproduce."

I was really tired. On the other side of my bedroom wall I could hear the sound of the evening news and the rattle of pots and pans. Someone somewhere was frying steak. I heard a smoke detector go off and then fall silent with a throttled sound. I woke with a start at the bottom of a nod.

I stumbled over to the bed. "I'm going to sleep. Move over," I muttered. Phoebe shifted herself to one side of the air above the bed. I kicked off my shoes and lay down on top of the blankets. I pulled an afghan over me and curled up into a ball, my head on my favorite lumpy pillow. "'Night," I managed to say before I disappeared into sleep.

I woke up when the first grey light started to creep around the bedroom. My bra dug into my back. My clothes had pressed my skin into strange wrinkles. My cold feet stuck out beyond the edge of the afghan. I heard a faint scrabbling noise. I rolled onto my side and saw Phoebe's back where she sat at my desk. She was leaning over, drawing something with a pencil. She turned the pencil upside down and there was the sound of furious erasing. A pause. Pencil scratched on paper again.

I swung my feet onto the gritty floor and padded over to the desk. Phoebe was concentrating so hard she didn't hear me. All over the page of the legal pad, my rectangles were filled with tiny figures. Phoebe was a pretty good artist, although her technique was a little old-fashioned; her style was middle Renaissance.

She stopped, then twisted around to look up at me. I leaned over her shoulder, close enough to feel the slight coolness emanating from her. The scenes were very small and detailed. In one row of boxes I could see the story's separate scenes as though it were a comic book: Jo-Jo on his knees in his room, Jo-Jo and a figure in a nun's habit. And another scene that we hadn't written yet—Jo-Jo on a stage.

Blanche's story was three scenes joined: a triptych whose large center panel featured Blanche and Shaquita standing in stylized fashion next to each other, facing slightly outward, their hands folded as if in prayer. Behind them Phoebe had drawn in the flat fields and tall pine forests of eastern North Carolina. In the smaller scene to the left, Shaquita and Bernard held hands, their faces turned away from each other. The scene to the right showed Blanche and Ervin, standing side by side, staring straight out at me. In Ervin's hand was a fishing pole; he wore a battered baseball cap. Blanche held a smoking cigarette. On the table next to her was a bottle of Paul Masson wine.

"It looks like an altarpiece," I said, examining the scenes of Blanche's story more closely.

"Well, that's the style I'm familiar with," said Phoebe.

"I like that you put Blanche and Shaquita in the center."

"It's really their story," she said.

"Where's Carla?" I asked.

"The box with her father is over here." In one of the rectangles Phoebe had drawn the scene with Carla's drunken father. "But I mostly put her on the edge of the paper since these are her boxes." I hadn't noticed before that Phoebe had filled in the margins of the paper with elaborate patterns like those in an illuminated manuscript (another of her early influences, I guessed). The patterns were of Carla, and Frederico, and Angelica, and Carla's apartment, and the bar, all intertwined with curling vines and gargoyles.

"Gargoyles?" I asked.

"It's part of the style," Phoebe said.

The rest of the rectangles that filled the page held scenes I didn't recognize. "What are those of?" I asked.

"Other stories," said Phoebe. "I don't know their titles yet."

There were men and women dancing and fighting, leopards and dogs, birds and mountains. There were mirrors and rainbows and setting suns and thistles. Phoebe's universe looked like an apartment building full of separate lives.

I opened the blind. We both squinted at the sudden bright sunlight that streamed in. Down in the parking lot, my neighbors were streaming from their doors, getting into their cars, and driving off in different directions in a hurry. The rows of blank windows in the buildings around me looked like rectangles on a page.

"I gotta go to work," I said. I couldn't quite remember what I usually did once I got there. I threw on clean clothes, grabbed my purse, and jogged down the stairs. Phoebe didn't follow.

I arrived at work just in time to attend a seminar on online documentation that I had completely forgotten about. I sat in the back of the auditorium. Halfway through the lecture, I started drawing in the margins of my legal pad. My style was more modern than Phoebe's. I drew tall Carla standing in the top margin.

FREDERICO LEAVES CARLA'S apartment that afternoon, but not before he has brushed her cheek with his lips and his fuzzy dark mustache. She listens to him *click-click-click* down the metal stairs outside her door. The sun is setting over the harbor; the empty warehouses on her street are struck with a clear golden light. Carla touches her cheek and watches the warehouses until the sun sets and they turn to dusky grey. Her cup is half-full of cold tea. She turns on the stove to boil more water.

The little figure of Jo-Jo is dry now. Carla paints white and black around his face, so that it looks like he's wearing a nun's habit. She leans him in a corner of an empty box. She watches him, waiting for the little figure to tell his story to her. Eventually, he does.

GROWNUP JO-JO BEGINS HIS act on the nightclub stage dressed only in snow-white briefs that glow against his black skin; he is clearly a man. He walks like a man, talks like a man. Still wearing the briefs, he pulls on pantyhose, reaches behind his back to fasten a padded bra, slides a silken slip over his head. His voice turns into a husky contralto. As he clothes himself, he talks about his childhood in Buffalo.

"There's a poem called 'The Hound of Heaven' that the nuns would read to us," he whispers. "It's about how you can run but you can't hide from God. I took it to mean that you can run but you can't hide from what you are.

"But," he continues as he wriggles into a red satin dress, "what am I?" He sits down at the edge of the stage and pulls high heels onto his big feet. He stands, cocks his hip, places a hand with long fingernails on it. For some reason, we didn't notice the fingernails when he stood before us almost naked as a man. He sits down at a dressing table that has been wheeled out onto a corner of the stage. Carefully, carefully, he makes himself up, still talking to us. His eyelashes grow long and elegant. "Is this what a woman is?" he asks us. He points the lipstick at his lips. He purses them. "Or is this my picture of a woman?"

The wig is the last to go on. It is as black and glossy as Jo-Jo's skin. It falls from his head to his shoulders in long, loose curls. "I know women say I'm mocking them."

He stands before the audience in all his glory and waits until the hoots and catcalls die down. "But this is not what a woman is. This is the fabulous creature I invented myself to be."

He picks up a microphone from the dressing table. "I'm going to sing an old drag queen standard for you." He starts "Somewhere Over the Rainbow" with a whisper that moves into full voice. Jo-Jo has a pretty voice. It could be either a man's or a woman's.

CARLA PLACES A LITTLE DRESSING table on Jo-Jo's stage. She bends down to look into its mirror and touches her cheek again where Frederico's black mustache brushed against it.

I did everything I was supposed to that day, I think, but mostly my mind was with Jo-Jo. It was dusk again when I came home, as it was dusk in the apartment where Carla was building little boxes of the lives of our characters. I didn't see Phoebe at first. A faint glow emanated from the bedroom. I peeked through the door. Phoebe was staring at the blank wall, tapping the end of her pencil against the wooden desk.

"Writer's block?" I asked.

"I haven't been able to think of a damn thing all day."

"You should have come to work with me."

"Why? I don't want to write computer manuals."

I told her my vision of Carla, and Carla's vision of Jo-Jo. She looked a little put out.

"C'mon," I said. "It's Friday night. Let's go down to the Grill."

I assumed any social occasion for me would be a social occasion for Phoebe. I changed into my lesbian clothes. We got to the Grill a bit later than usual, or rather, I did, since Phoebe had vanished again. People were already on their second pitchers of beer. I rushed to catch up. I sat down next to Darlene, who could never resist joining us and had left control of the rest of the restaurant to the cook. I grabbed a sticky plastic cup and poured out the last of the pitcher. Darlene said, "I'd say I was glad to see you, except now I have to go get another one." She clapped me on the shoulder as she left for the bar. "Now tell everyone if you're a virgin."

"Hell, no," I said. "I lost my virginity twice."

"How'd you do that?" asked the woman across the table. "Get your hymen sewed back together?"

"Lost it the first time to a man and the second time to a woman."

They laughed. The woman across the table from me said, "You know, I still rate men on an attractiveness scale."

"Me, too," I said. "Gay men generally rank better than straight men."

Darlene had come back into the room with two full pitchers. "Do you rank women, too?" she asked.

"Different scale," I said. "Is-a-dyke, isn't-a-dyke, should-be-a-dyke-even-if-she-thinks-she-isn't."

"Only three rankings?"

"There's more. After they're sorted, then there are cute dykes, cute straight women, etcetera."

"Boy, this is becoming complicated," said the woman across from me.

"There's more." I was getting into this. "Someone can qualify as a cute dyke but then turn out to be a jerk, at which point she achieves a ranking of shouldn't-be-a-dyke."

"Like Martina's ex-girlfriend," someone said.

"She's definitely excommunicated."

There was a circle of women around the table; there was the faint din of rock-and-roll from the other side of the restaurant, where Darlene piped in music from some awful oldies station. She started to tell us about her ex-husband, PeeWee. "And there was a reason he was called that," she said, holding up her little finger. Maybe it was the beer, but I was happy that night, happier than I'd been in a long time. It had been a while since I'd been to Brigadoon—even though I still went to the Grill regularly, I had been holding myself apart. But on that night with kind Darlene and a bunch of other women, most of whom I didn't even know, I felt as though I was swimming in my old comfortable river again. I was so glad Beatrice wasn't there. I might have let myself miss her if I had seen her.

Happiness is simple. I kept forgetting that. Sadness is very complicated, but happiness is simple.

I lay in bed for a long time the next morning, drifting in and out of sleep. Suddenly, my covers disappeared.

"Hey!"

Phoebe had yanked the blankets and sheets onto the floor. "Get up," she said. "Write."

"Go away. Find another victim. I'm taking the day off."

"Your life's too short," she said. What did that mean? I curled up in a little ball, my arms over my head. I emitted a light snore that I thought was very convincing. Phoebe tickled the bottoms of my feet. I kicked at her.

"Leave me alone."

"Not for the rest of your life," she said. I didn't ask her how long that would be. Dying tragically young was starting to have a certain appeal.

I staggered out of bed and padded to the bathroom, then to the kitchen, where I cranked up the coffeemaker. While the coffee was brewing, I shuffled back to the bathroom and viewed the startled shape of my hair in the mirror. It was an accurate depiction of my inner state, so I didn't mess with it. I caught a flickered glimpse of Phoebe's reflection in the other room, which I would have thought interesting if I hadn't been pissed off. Phoebe couldn't be seen in mirrors.

"How does one describe the taste of beer?" she asked.

"Some people think it's bitter," I said as I left the bathroom.

"'Bitter.' Bitter tastes bad. Why do you drink so much of it?"

I poured myself a cup of coffee. "Because it makes cigarettes taste so good." So far Phoebe's primary sin was self-righteousness. I lit one and inhaled deeply. "Ah. This is the life." I observed Phoebe as she silently resolved not to let me get to her this time.

"Am I a lesbian?" she asked.

I had a startling thought. "Phoebe, I don't even know if you're a girl."

"I don't think I have a gender."

"Why do you have a girl's name?"

"You gave it to me when you were little, remember? It sort of sounded like Pinky, whom you named first, I might add."

"You mean you weren't always named Phoebe?"

"I usually didn't have a name, since my people didn't know I was there. A little boy called me Joe. I wasn't Joe for very long, since the little boy died when he was five. There was a nun in the twelfth century who had delusions of grandeur and thought I was the Archangel Gabriel."

She settled down at the table. "Tell me about lust," she said.

That got my attention.

"Do you feel desire?" I asked.

"I think I did."

"You think you did when?"

"Last night."

"Where were you last night?"

"Same place as you, of course. Until I followed what's-her-name home."

"Who?"

"I don't know. I didn't ask. I needed to find out about lust. It's the first one on my list of sins."

Phoebe was making me very uneasy. *Succubus* was the word that sprang to mind. *Incubus. Amanuensis*—no, that wasn't right. That was closer to what I was.

"Her body was different from yours," she said.

I was appalled but curious. "So how did it go?" I vaguely asked. "Are you sure you didn't get her name?"

"It was interesting," said Phoebe, "and yes, I'm sure I don't know who she was. It might have been more interesting if she had been awake."

Yeccchhh. "Phoebe, there are supposed to be two people involved, not just one."

"How could I know she'd fall asleep so fast?"

"She'd probably have run screaming from the room if she'd been awake and seen you."

"As it was, I had to elbow her angel out of the way. I told him I was on special assignment."

"And her angel bought that?"

"I doubt it. He was rather interested himself. He watched me pretty carefully."

This was awful. An army of predatory guardian angels. "Phoebe, if you want to be real, people have to have sex *with* you, not just you stealing sex from them."

"Lust is lust," she said stubbornly.

"Sins by themselves are just disembodied bad traits. You're already disembodied."

"When are you going to get together with somebody?" she asked. "You've been celibate for months."

"I've been busy," I said. "And I've lacked privacy."

"You never needed privacy before."

"I didn't know I was being watched."

"Not that it was all that interesting." She seemed to think of something. She laughed to herself.

"What's so funny?"

"Nothing. Nothing at all. Just a little memory." Her mouth moved and she looked away, trying to keep a straight face. Incubus. Succubus. Doppelgänger. Pain in the ass.

I was standing in front of the kitchen counter pouring myself a second cup when I heard an invisible someone whisper in my ear.

"Don't be afraid," it said.

"Get away from me."

"I'm not going to hurt you."

"Go experiment on someone else."

I swung my elbow out against the whisper and encountered what felt like spiderwebs.

"Oof!" said Phoebe. "Okay, okay. You don't have to be so rough." She reappeared looking misshapen. She arranged herself back into her usual form. I worried about what she would do while I slept. I couldn't stay awake forever.

"Listen," I said, "we need to agree on something here. I can't spend all my time worrying that my guardian angel's going to molest me in the night. You want to be real, right?"

She barely nodded.

"Or do you want to spend all eternity as a scary phantom?"

She looked intrigued. "What are you saying?" she asked.

"The other person has to know you're there." It occurred to me that Phoebe didn't have a clear idea of how to go about being human. She depended on me for advice. Angels were not nearly as smart as they were cracked up to be. "Find someone who's attracted to *you*." She looked at me wistfully. "Someone you don't already know," I hastily added.

"Impossible," said Phoebe, and disappeared.

I brought the coffee into the bedroom. I crawled around on the floor until I discovered my other pack of cigarettes under the bed, where Phoebe had probably tossed them in the hopes that I would forget I smoked. At my desk, I dumped the overflowing ashtray into a trashcan. I lit a cigarette. I picked my favorite fountain pen from the mason jar. I pulled off the cap and began to write on the legal pad in front of me.

IT'S TIME FOR CARLA TO GO to work. She dresses in a white silk blouse and black billowing pants. She puts on earrings in the shapes of hearts and stars. She throws on her magenta cape and strides out the door and down the metal stairs. She climbs into her enormous ancient Buick and smokes down the street.

It's a busy Saturday night. By the end of the evening, a line of designated drivers and their dates are sitting drunk at the bar. One of the designated drivers stares at Carla's boxes in front of the mirror. "Gee," she says, "it's like a little TV. Only it doesn't move."

"Yes, it does," says the one sitting next to her. The first one looks startled and then bursts into gales of helpless laughter. The other one joins her. Carla would like to throw a blanket over the heads of both shrieking women as though they were canaries and tell them it's time to shut up and go to sleep. She wipes the sticky counter around them. Almost closing time, thank God. Behind the squeals she hears a *click-*

click-click. She looks up. Frederico stands next to the door. He smiles and waves.

"Closing time," Carla says to the two women.

"Who's the designated driver?" they ask, and start laughing again.

"Do you want me to call a taxi?"

"What?" says one of the women. She stares at Carla's lips as though she were lipreading. "What?"

"Taxi?"

"No, my name's Sue." They laugh some more. Carla dials the number for Yellow Cab.

"He'll be here in a few minutes," she says.

"What? What? Look, the little TV's moving again." They take their eyes off the lower half of Carla's face and wobble their vision over to the box until the cab comes. Carla guides them out the door and locks it behind them. She flips the sign to CLOSED.

"I thought they'd never leave."

"What?" says Frederico. He's sitting at the bar, staring at the little box.

"Stop it. Or I'll throw a blanket over your head."

"Would you like to step out for a drink?"

"Thanks, I can't stand the sight of any more alcohol or the people who drink it. Why don't you come home with me? I'll fix some tea."

"Yes," he says.

Carla can see the blinking headlight of Frederico's motorcycle behind her as she steers the Buick home. When she comes to a stop in front of her loft, she hears the sputtering motorcycle pull up behind her. In his round white helmet, Frederico looks like a tiny moon man wearing black leather. He sticks the helmet under his arm and trots with Carla up to her apartment.

"Don't turn on the light," he says. The streetlight casts the black grid of the windowpane onto the white wall in the kitchen. With the color gone from Carla's golden apartment, it looks like a ghost of itself. She takes off her magenta cape, which now appears black. Frederico unzips his leather jacket.

The stove burner's ring glows red in this silver place. Carla arranges the tea things on a tray and brings them to the table where the unfinished boxes are and where Frederico is sitting. His skin is very white, his hair very black. A silver mist of steam rises up from the cups. They can hear each other sip the tea.

Carla puts her hand out flat on the table. After a moment, Frederico covers her hand with his. His palm is warm and slightly damp. Carla wiggles her fingers a little, and he smiles.

"I'm glad you came over," she says.

"I am glad to be here with you."

Carla feels as though she is in a sphere of glass. If she moves too quickly, or says the wrong thing, the glass will break. Before this day she has thought of Frederico only as Angelica's brother and, there-fore, her—Carla's—friend. She has not dreamt about him awake or asleep. She has not wanted him before today. Where they are now has no history, does not make any particular sense.

She turns her palm upward to let their hands grasp each other. Frederico looks solemn as he traces with his finger the vein that runs along the inside of Carla's wrist and her inner arm. His finger describes little circles on her inner arm. His finger goes back down to the palm of her hand. He holds her hand as he gets up from his stool and walks around to her side of the table. While Carla is sitting on the stool they are the same height. She gets up, still holding his hand, and they walk together to the futon under the wall of little boxes. They move very carefully in the delicate white air of the streetlight.

PHOEBE POPPED INTO VIEW next to my elbow.

"The air in heaven is white," she said.

"Where does the light come from?"

She shrugged. "I don't know. I never thought about it before. Nobody says much in heaven."

"You and the other angels don't hang out between lives and gos-sip?"

"No, it's not like here. It's like Carla's glass sphere. It's so beautiful you're terrified of breaking it by doing or saying the wrong thing. It's a relief to come back down to earth and not be afraid to breathe."

I thought of Carla and Frederico. The streetlight shines on their bare skin as they move slowly over each other's bodies. They whisper.

"What are you thinking?" asked Phoebe.

"About Carla."

"Write it down."

INSIDE THE APARTMENT, IT's warm enough to lie naked on the bed without a blanket. Frederico seems to be listening even as he is looking closely at the skin of her back, her breasts, her stomach. He smoothes her soft skin with his hands. Frederico's body is small and hard. There is a down of black hair on his back and chest. She touches his back. He moves like a cat against her hand. They make love to each other carefully, as though inspired by someone outside of themselves, by the place the silver light comes from. Afterwards they sleep. Before she falls into her dreams, Carla sits up to find the blanket. Frederico murmurs and tries to pull her back down next to him. Carla falls to his side with the blanket and covers them up. They sleep curled around each other. Carla can hear Frederico's breath brush against his mustache.

"I DIDN'T KNOW IT WAS LIKE that," said Phoebe.

"Sometimes."

IN THE EARLY MORNING, WHILE it is still dark, Carla awakens in the tangle that she and Frederico have made. Frederico's arm lies across her breasts. Carla slips out from under his arm and puts on the old plaid bathrobe that belonged to her father. She goes to the table where the unfinished boxes are. She can see the figures clearly. The streetlight is still enough. She picks up an empty box from the floor. Frederico, who is a little bit awake, watches Carla from the bed. Her hair is a dark mass. He can just see her white breast exposed by the opening in her bathrobe. Her shoulders are broad; she could encircle the top of the table with her two arms.

As she drives home from the mill that afternoon, Blanche passes flat green fields bordered by trees so tall they look like a mountain range in the distance. The white-green grass of the fields shimmers in the heat. Her car doesn't have air conditioning. The trailer has a window unit that's wheezing loudly when she walks in the door. The kids are arguing out on the back porch.

Blanche shouts through the closed back door. "Shannon, Joshua, Brian—quit fighting and get in here. Have you done your chores? Whose turn is it to feed the dog?" The children push at each other as they jostle their way inside. They don't bother to argue with their mother after she gets home from work, although Shannon makes a token effort.

"It's Brian's turn, Ma."

"'Snot," says Brian. "'Snot, 'snot, 'snot."

Blanche grabs Brian by the arm and turns him around. "Don't think I don't know what you're saying, young man. Now get out there and feed that dog." He rushes back out into the hot afternoon, which is safer just now than in the trailer. Joshua picks up their toys from the carpet of the living room floor. Shannon starts washing dishes.

"Where'd them dirty bowls come from? You better not have eaten all the ice cream." Blanche looks in the freezer. In the corner of the ice cream carton is a teaspoon's worth of Rocky Road.

"We didn't eat all of it, Ma," says Shannon.

"Your daddy ain't going to be too happy when he gets home and finds his ice cream gone."

Blanche pulls the makings of dinner from the refrigerator and tosses them on the table.

"Can we have fish sticks?" asks Joshua.

"Meatloaf," says Blanche. Joshua makes a face that she just misses seeing. Blanche pushes past Shannon to wash her hands at the sink. She settles down at the kitchen table and starts mixing hamburger, breadcrumbs, and catsup in a bowl with her hands.

"Ugh," says Shannon.

"You'll eat it," says Blanche, her hands covered with a thin layer of raw meat and crumbs and ketchup. She slaps the mixture into a baking dish, shoves it into the oven, and turns the oven on.

"It's too hot to cook," whines Shannon as a last resort. "Why can't we go to Arby's?"

"'Cause we're poor, that's why." Blanche opens a big can of green beans and dumps them into a pan. She pulls out a loaf of white bread and puts it on the table. "Joshua, set the plates and glasses out. Your daddy'll be home soon." Blanche brushes against the walls as she walks swiftly down the hall to the master bedroom. She pulls off her linty workclothes and slips on a pink shift that's loose enough not to touch her anywhere. She squeezes into the tiny bathroom to throw water on her face. Brian has come back into the trailer. She can hear the kids bickering in the living room. She freshens her lipstick and sprays a shot of hairspray onto the top of her hair.

"Peee-yooo." Brian runs by the open bathroom door, holding his nose.

Blanche steps out of the bathroom fast enough to swat his butt with her hairbrush. "You hush your mouth." They hear the rumble of Ervin's truck outside and smell the exhaust seeping through the walls. The truck door slams.

"Wash your hands," yells Blanche as she leaves the bathroom. The kids cluster around the sink like bees. They shove one another's hands from underneath the faucet. The door pops open and Ervin walks in. He flips his baseball cap off and hangs it on a hook next to the door.

"Dinner ready?" he asks.

"Will be by the time you clean up." Blanche is pulling the meatloaf out of the oven. When Ervin comes out of the bathroom, they are all seated at the table. Joshua and Brian kick at each other.

"We got any pickles?" asks Ervin as he sits down. Blanche gets up and opens the refrigerator. She grabs a jar of dill cubes and sets it out. They eat rapidly, in silence. The hot food makes them sweat. Ervin's can of beer sits next to his glass of iced tea. Brian wiggles in his chair when he is finished and gives his mother a pleading look.

"You're excused," Blanche says to him. All the children jump out of their chairs and scurry toward the back door. "Shannon, finish those dishes," Blanche calls after her. Shannon stops at the back door and slumps over to the sink. The boys dash out into the hot light. Ervin sets his crumpled paper napkin beside his plate.

"Truck's running rough. I'm going to give it a look." He puts his baseball cap back on and pulls a beer from the six-pack in the refrigerator before he goes out.

Blanche lights a Salem and keeps on sitting at the table. In front of her lies the wreckage of dinner. A corner of the meatloaf remains in the baking pan. She picks at it. She pulls off half a slice of bread. Shannon picks up the almost empty meatloaf pan.

"Leave it," says Blanche. She chews and swallows the meatloaf, and then takes another puff on her cigarette. The smoke gathers in a flat cloud against the low ceiling. The air conditioner in the living room window rumbles and wheezes.

"I'm done, Ma," Shannon says.

"Go on, then." The back door slams behind Shannon. "Don't slam the door," says Blanche. She can just barely hear the drip of the kitchen faucet over the noise of the air conditioner.

CARLA PULLS HER ROBE AROUND her. She goes to the enormous window through which the streetlight is shining. She crouches down next to a big cardboard box. She can smell the yeasty scent of sex coming from her body. Her vagina is a little bit sore. She rummages around in the box with one hand, while the other hand holds the front of her robe closed. She pulls out a rag doll with stuffed arms and a round head.

Carla stuffs the doll into the empty box on the table. She puts four other tiny plastic figures near the doll. The figures run in a circle around the doll, who stands motionless in the center.

"THAT'S BLANCHE," SAID PHOEBE.

"Right."

"What's this about sex smelling?"

"You didn't notice when you snuck into that poor anonymous woman's bed?"

"I guess I didn't take a sniff."

"Everything has a scent."

"It does?" Phoebe inhaled deeply through her nose. "I don't smell anything."

I looked around for something strong. There was that hamburger casserole that had been in the refrigerator too long. "Try this," I said. When I popped the top of the Tupperware that held the hamburger I was almost knocked out by the odor.

Phoebe stuck her nose in and sniffed hard. "Nothing," she said.

"Nothing at all?"

She looked as though she were listening for music she couldn't quite hear. "A little."

"Whew." I couldn't stand it any longer. I dumped the ancient casserole into the trash and closed the lid. I opened a can of the cheap tuna that tastes just like cat food. "Now?" I asked.

"Flat?"

This was progress, maybe. I had a little bottle of patchouli oil on my dresser. I pulled the stopper and waved it under her nose. She sneezed.

She said, "When you ask me what something smells like, I can't describe it because I haven't smelled anything before. Patchouli smells like you've ripped open a feather pillow and shaken it out. The hamburger casserole smells like the time we couldn't go outside for two weeks because it was raining and you had bronchitis."

I pulled a sweater from the closet. I was sure my clothes smelled smoky, even though I couldn't detect it

"Here." I held it out for Phoebe's nasal inspection. "This is Blanche's trailer."

Phoebe held the wool against her face and inhaled hard. "Ah," she said, "it smells like frustration."

I wondered about something. I leaned over to Phoebe, close enough to feel the coolness of her glassy skin against my face. I breathed slowly in and out through my nose. She smelled like an approaching rainstorm, at the point where the air changes from a sultry afternoon where nothing happens to a feeling that change is coming.

AT HER KITCHEN TABLE, BLANCHE hears the kids yelling and the dog yapping out the back, and the clang of Ervin's wrench falling against the side of the truck out front. She drums her fingers on the table. She can't relax.

"THAT'S A VERY CROWDED LITTLE box," says Frederico. He has come up behind Carla. He entwines his fingers in the sash of her bathrobe and leans around her. His head presses against her arm. Ervin and the kids and big Blanche are all jammed into the box that is their trailer. "What are you going to do with the dark woman?" The figure of Shaquita lies on the table next to the box.

BLANCHE SLIPS ON A BLOUSE and a pair of slacks. She steps out of the trailer. "I'm going to get the backseat of the car looked at, where Joshua stuck a knife in it," she says to Ervin's back where he's leaning under the hood of the truck. "Watch the kids."

He grunts. The truck radio is playing. A beer can balances on the top of the metal frame next to his head.

Blanche drives down the highway on her way to the auto upholstery man. She spots his white hand-painted sign and pulls into his yard. A lone dog comes cringing, its tail between its legs, from the pine woods behind the house. No one else is around. Blanche waits for a minute, then pulls back out onto the highway. The colored settlement is down a dirt road somewhere along here. She almost drives past it before she recognizes it.

Without thinking too much, she turns down the long road, past grey Spanish moss hanging from the trees. Trash is scattered along the side: beer cans and a sprung sofa halfway in the ditch. This is where people take their big junk when they don't want to pay the fee at the dump.

She comes up on Niggertown before she expects to. A tarpaper house sits close to the road, with a design in the paper painted to make it look like cinderblocks. A real cinderblock house sits next to it. Then a field. Then a cluster of trailers. Chickens step delicately in and out of the door of one of them. Some kids are jumping around in the muddy water of the ditch. Blanche slows down. They stare at her. A little girl shouts words in a high voice that Blanche can't understand. Her friend pushes at her and they both laugh and watch Blanche float slowly by. Across from the cluster of trailers is a squat white church with a crooked steeple. Behind the church, gravestones are tilted in the sandy soil. Blanche knows they all can see her—from their gardens, their black windows, maybe even from inside the church where she's stopped to turn around again and go back through the town. Georgetown. Blanche tries not to think the other name in front of them. She drives back past those kids. In her rearview mirror she sees one of them throw a clod of dirt after the car. Is Shaquita watching her from one of those dark windows? Blanche can't imagine fat white Bernard in this place.

"YOU EVER WISH YOU WERE invisible?" asked Phoebe.

"All the time," I said. "I'd love to see what goes on when I'm not around. Like, does the furniture dance in my living room at night?"

Phoebe just smiled.

"Well? Does it?"

"I can't say," she said.

I tapped my pen on the legal pad. "Blanche would very much like to be invisible right now."

"It's not all it's cracked up to be," said Phoebe. "But the worst thing is being untouchable: nothing can touch me and I can touch nothing." She faded in and out. "I heard a baby crying once," she said. "I was on my way to your birth, as a matter of fact. I had slowed down to take a look around the place where I was going to spend the first years of your life. It's a pretty town, isn't it? Brick sidewalks, boxwoods, a drugstore, a five-and-dime. It was like a picture in a calendar.

"I heard a baby crying. For a minute I was confused and I thought it was you, but I was a mile from the hospital, much too far away to hear you. The crying was close by, but inside of something or behind a wall. There was a row of metal trash cans along a brick sidewalk, beside a sunlit, peaceful street. The sound was coming from the can on the end. I couldn't lift the lid but I could pass through the silver metal to look inside. A newborn baby girl lay on a pile of rags inside the can, crying as though her heart were breaking. Where was her angel? I looked up at the sky and saw nothing, heard no answer. I tried to comfort the baby, but she couldn't hear me because I was not her angel. I tried once again to open the lid of the can. Of course I couldn't move it. I flew up and down the streets, peering into the windows of all the pretty houses. A cat lying on a rug in the sunlight saw me and raised its head, but there was no one else. I floated paralyzed above the can, torn between you and this baby who did not belong to me. I wanted to choose again."

She glanced at me and looked away. "It's not that I didn't want to be with you, but this baby had no one. You do understand, don't you?"

"Of course," I said.

"I wanted to at least be able to stroke the few strands of hair from her forehead, to hold her close until she died. I wanted more than that, though—I wanted the strength to lift the lid of the trash can, to pick the baby up and carry her to the hospital where someone could care for her. I pleaded to be able to do this, but there was no answer."

"What happened to the baby?" I asked.

"I don't know," said Phoebe. "You were born. I was at your side."

I imagined I heard a baby's faint cries in the distance.

"I think of that baby as your twin," she said.

I shuddered for my lost sister.

She said, "For the first time it occurred to me that I wasn't real, in this world at least. I'm a figment of God's imagination."

I reached out to put my warm hand on her cool arm. "Does God know how real you're getting to be?"

"I don't know what God knows," Phoebe said. "He didn't seem to know about the baby in the trash can."

This was too depressing. I started writing about Carla, who seemed like a pretty happy person.

WITH THE SASH OF HER BATHROBE, Frederico draws Carla away from the table and toward the bed. He slips the robe from her strong shoulders before they lie back down together.

"AGAIN?" SAID PHOEBE.

"That's what you wanted to hear about, isn't it?"

WHEN CARLA NEXT WAKES UP, sunlight has turned the apartment golden. Frederico is sitting on the edge of the bed, easing on his black boots.

"I am late already for rehearsal."

Carla pulls him back down onto the bed so she can feel his smooth leather jacket against her naked skin.

"Tonight?" asks Frederico.

"Yes. Let's go dancing."

She lets him out of her embrace. They smile at each other before Frederico *click-click-clicks* across the wooden floor to the door and then down the metal stairs. She listens to the rumble of his motorcycle fade away. Carla gets up to stand tall and naked in front of the big window. She spreads her arms wide in the warm yellow sunlight streaming onto her from above the empty street. Dust motes sparkle in the air around her.

Sunday is her day off. She throws a blanket over the rumpled white sheets of her bed. She dresses all in black: a black turtleneck and black jeans. The boxes lie waiting for her on the work table. The sunlight shines into the box that holds Jo-Jo.

It's three o'clock in the afternoon. The club reeks of spilled beer and stale cigarette smoke. The walls need repainting, which you can't tell at night when it's crowded and the lights hanging from the ceiling are swirling and flashing.

Jo-Jo says, "Man, this place looks like a dog in the daytime."

Shirley, the bartender, is wiping down the bar at the far end.

"You need another drink?"

"No, honey, I'm just talking to myself." He tilts his head back to empty his wine glass and sets a quarter down on the bar. Shirley looks at him. Jo-Jo adds another quarter. "Getting pretty hard to find conversation in the middle of the day. People just don't drink the way they used to, and I have to tell you, it's a damn shame for social discourse. What can they be doing all day? Working?"

A few hours from now, Shirley and three men will be sloshing liquor into glasses as fast as they can while they try to hear the next order over the noise of the crowd. Jo-Jo watches her as she adds water to the bottles arranged in neat rows along the back of the bar.

"Didn't your mother ever tell you it's rude to stare?" Shirley says without turning around.

"Frankly, it never occurred to my mama there was anything bad about rudeness. Did it ever occur to you that it's rude to put water in people's drinks when they didn't ask for it?"

"It's not rude unless they don't know about it. And you'd have to be a fool not to figure out what we do."

"The Lord protects fools and little children, I guess."

"I hope he takes care of little children, but fools that get protected just stay fools."

Jo-Jo lights another cigarette from the butt of the one he's been smoking. Shirley says, "Can I bum one?"

"Oh, sure, sure. Here you go." He hands her the one he's just lit and lights another for himself. "I thought you quit."

"I quit buying them."

"Sounds like you won't stop smoking until the rest of the world goes cold turkey."

"I'll really quit pretty soon." The new smoke floats up to the ceiling and hovers there. "You doing Judy Garland again tonight?"

"It is *not* Judy Garland."

"I don't get you queens. Anybody who wears pantyhose when they don't have to is just plain nuts. Poor Judy must be spinning in her grave with all these faggots wearing their mothers' dresses and screeching her songs."

"Ouch," says Jo-Jo. "I'm cut to the quick."

"I'm sorry, Jo-Jo." Shirley pats his hand. "Would a watered-down drink make you feel better?"

"You don't do that to the wine, do you?'

"Naw. We just give you the cheapest stuff we can find."

"Ain't that the truth. You can pour me a glass of your faux red if you want me to feel better."

"This isn't on the house, now."

"Is it happy hour yet?"

"Fifteen minutes," says Shirley.

"C'mon now, cut me just a little slack."

"Okay. Half price, just this once. Don't ask me again."

"Never again, baby, never again." The raw wine sets Jo-Jo's teeth on edge.

"Judy Garland was a dyke, you know," Shirley says.

"That right?" Jo-Jo is intrigued.

"Her and Ingrid Bergman kept company."

"*Really?* I've never heard that one."

"Lotta stars are dykes. Julie Andrews, Whitney Houston."

"Now I *have* heard about ol' Whitney. And I believe it, too. The woman's got to be hiding *something* underneath the blandness."

"Come to think of it, that's an example of a dyke doing drag."

"There you go," says Jo-Jo. "You say you never feel the urge to dress up?"

"I take a walk on the wild side now and then."

"How's that?"

"Dress like a man. See if I can pass."

"And do you?"

"Not around here, where everybody cross-dresses anyway. I can pass in a straight bar."

"The women ever come on to you?"

"Yeah. They do." Shirley blows her smoke straight up to the ceiling and smiles.

"Sounds like a tricky situation."

"I manage. Just like you."

"Oh, my." Jo-Jo fans himself with his hand. "Miss Shirl, I had no idea. One of these days we're going to have to compare our tricks of the trade."

"You know people are not always what they seem to be."

THE BLUE SKY OUTSIDE MY WINDOW had a golden cast to it, like it might be afternoon. I got up out of my straight-backed chair and stretched. My joints made popping noises. Phoebe winced. "Doesn't it hurt when you do that?" she asked.

"Feels great. Let's get out of here. Hell of a way to spend a Saturday." I lit a cigarette and, with the cigarette in my mouth, pulled my T-shirt over my head.

"How in the world do you manage not to set yourself on fire?" she asked.

"Years of practice," I muttered from inside the smoke-filled T-shirt. My eyes stung. I went to my bureau drawer and pulled out another T-shirt very similar to the one I had taken off.

I walked out into a late afternoon in spring. My birthday was coming up soon. The thought depressed me; as far as I was concerned, birthdays, not cigarettes, were nails in my coffin. I thought of my long-lost twin, whose birthday might be the same as mine. "Do you think the baby in the trash can is still alive?" I asked Phoebe.

Phoebe shrugged. Her repertoire of human gestures had expanded. "Maybe we could find her."

"Do you really want to meet a person without an angel?"

"What does it mean that she has no angel?"

"She'd be a lost soul. They're dangerous, like bulls in emotional china shops. She'd be floundering around, searching for something she can't find, demanding compensation for a loss she doesn't remember. I'd stay away from lost souls if I were you. They're not our concern."

"Couldn't we save her?"

"No one can save her. I'm sorry, but that's the way it is. Either you have a guardian angel or there's no help for you."

"What kind of God would orchestrate such a thing?" I asked her.

"In my opinion, He is either cruel or stupid."

We were so angry at Phoebe's boss we didn't even glance heavenward at this latest blasphemy.

"Serial killers are lost souls," Phoebe said. "They want to steal grace from people by taking their lives."

"Phoebe, have you ever seen God?"

She thought for longer than a minute. "You don't see much in heaven; it's a pretty transcendent state."

"So who's running the show?"

"Maybe nobody is. Maybe that's the problem."

"Is my twin going to go to hell?"

"Maybe she's there now," said Phoebe ambiguously.

I eyed the people walking by us. "Do you see any serial killers?" I whispered out of the corner of my mouth.

Phoebe glanced at the passersby. "No. They have angels."

The people were walking so close together it didn't seem that there could be any room for guardian angels between them. "I guess you would call them psychopaths," I said. "They don't all kill, but they're missing some connectedness to the rest of us."

My association with Phoebe was making me realize that the world was run according to a completely different set of rules from the ones I had been brought up to believe. The rules we hypothesized were crude abstractions for the real thing. There was a heaven, but you didn't see God there. What we called Original Sin had nothing to do with Adam and everything to do with some poor soul's luck of the draw; if you didn't have an angel when you were born, too bad for you. I was right when I was a little kid and believed that angels were the only characters in the catechism you could trust. "I bet there's no Holy Spirit, either," I said.

"I don't know where you people got that bird idea," Phoebe said.

"Human beings like to think in metaphors," I answered. The world now seemed a very cold place. I had been an atheist for years, but the confirmation that God might be nonexistent left me chilled. Angels were the only noncorporeal beings left, and, if Phoebe was any indication, their behavior was a little dicey. Nobody was minding the store. "Nobody here but us," I said.

"That's enough," said Phoebe. "We don't need anybody else."

"We hope," I said.

"There's still grace," she said. "It's not a bird, but it's there. There's still change, which may be the same thing as grace."

"Change is grace?" I asked.

"Yes," said Phoebe. "To change is to be born."

"Being born would make you human, wouldn't it? Is that why you want to change?"

"You, too," said Phoebe. "You, too."

By now we had walked a long way. Or rather, I had done the walking and Phoebe had done the floating. We had come beyond the sidewalks to where there were vacant spaces sprouting wild grasses and saplings. "Teach me to fly," I said.

"I can't do that."

"Why not?"

"Humans aren't supposed to fly."

"Now you're a stickler for rules? Angels aren't supposed to hop into strangers' beds either."

"Besides," said Phoebe, "I don't know how to teach you. We don't have gravity to contend with the way you do."

"Try," I said.

In the vacant lot in front of us, the wind blew the golden grasses this way and that. The grass came up to my chest when I walked into it. "It's going to be hard to get a running start in this stuff," I said.

"You don't run from gravity. You float into yourself."

The wind made a hushing sound all around us. My arms felt hemmed in by the moving grasses, which scratched slightly against my bare skin. Phoebe was a few feet away. Only her head was visible. "Watch me," she said. Without moving her arms, Phoebe slowly went straight up. She rose until she was a dot in the sky. The dot vanished, and she popped up next to me.

"How did you get down here so fast?"

"We'll learn astral projection some other day. Flying is easy; you just think it."

Right. I reminded myself that Phoebe had some difficulty putting one foot in front of the other on the ground. I thought flying. An image of me swooping like a swallow came into my mind. Wrong. I thought floating and got an image of the Goodyear blimp. I thought of the way angels seemed to move between the air and the light that shone on the air. Then I had the sensation that I was inside a thin layer of glass that moved the way I moved, the way glass does not. The hushing of the wind on the grasses became a little fainter. I looked down at my hand, which seemed to glow slightly. I waved it back and forth in front of my face to see if it would leave trails of light. A little bit, perhaps. I thought of the blue sky above me. The light of the sun seemed to lift me up until my heels were in the air and the toes of my boots scraped the ground. I turned to call to Phoebe to make sure she saw, and I fell back to earth with a thud.

"Ouch," I said.

Phoebe was examining blue chicory flowers and didn't notice.

"What's the matter?" she said absently. She was counting the petals, to what purpose I couldn't imagine.

"I flew."

"No, you didn't." Her tone was matter-of-fact.

"I did." My skin still felt a little glassy. I touched my arm to see if I could feel the hairs on it. I could, but the skin beneath them felt smoother and cooler than usual. "Feel my arm." I held my bare arm out to her. Phoebe's cool fingers went *dot-dot-dot* on my skin. She shrugged.

"Feels the same to me."

"My skin is smoother." I touched my arm again, but this time my skin was as rough and warm as always.

"This isn't going to work," Phoebe said. She watched me over the top of the grass. I tried to bring back the angel feeling I had had.

"Stop staring. I can't concentrate," I said.

"You need a witness, don't you?"

I thought of myself as an angel, with skin of glass and hair that glowed. I thought of my toes just brushing the ground. "I know what the problem is," I said. "I'm wearing shoes. Angels don't wear shoes." I sat down in the dark jungle of stems and untied my hiking boots. I took off my socks, too. Gingerly, I stood on the damp earth. My feet were pale and tender. I felt my heels sink slightly into the ground. My skin was like glass, I told myself. Gravity was a concept I could not grasp.

I held my arms out slightly from my sides. I could feel it, the space between the wind and the light of the setting sun. My heels lifted from the ground. The sound of the wind grew fainter. I looked out over the field and it was as though it was under very clear water. There was nothing between me and it, and yet there was: something like glass. I could no longer feel the wind on my skin but, in return, I was lifted higher above the grass, until my toes brushed the tops of the grain-laden heads. I was afraid to turn to see if Phoebe was still watching, or if she had gone back to her important business of petal-counting. "*Ssshhhhh, sssshhhhhh, shhhhhhh,*" the wind said.

In the place where I floated, I could barely hear the sounds of the real world. It was almost silent, except for a haunting silver note that came from far above me. I tried to take a breath. There was no air. I tried to move my arms to break out of the glass sphere that held me. This was like a dream from which I couldn't awaken. Did I need to breathe? I wasn't sure. I breathed in as hard as I could. The wind broke through the glass and I tumbled to the ground, grabbing at the air as I fell. The damp earth felt good against my bottom. I understood Phoebe's lust for physical sensation. I touched the rough stalks of the grass that swung in the air above my head and felt the wind blow through my hair. Phoebe floated into view.

"Well?" she asked.

"Did you see me?"

"No," she said, but I could tell she was lying.

"Yes, you did."

"Yes, I did. So how was it?"

"Kind of glassy," I said. She nodded. "I couldn't breathe, but I guess I didn't need to breathe, huh?" She shrugged.

"Did you like it?"

"I'm not sure." This was news to myself because I'd been so jealous of Phoebe's talents. "Is the music always turned on?"

"What music?" she asked.

"That note. It's coming from up there." I pointed at the sky.

Phoebe closed her eyes and listened. "Oh, yeah. That," she said. "You mean you don't hear it all the time?"

I shook my head.

"What do you hear?" She looked genuinely puzzled.

"Oh, a little of this and a little of that. Everything, I guess, except what you hear."

"I've heard that note for thousands of years," she said.

"Doesn't it get on your nerves?"

"It's louder in heaven. It's the only thing we hear in heaven. The closer we come to earth, the fainter it grows."

This sounded dreadful to me: a high-pitched whine you could never turn off. "What if you stuck your fingers in your ears?"

"Why would I want to do that? It's part of me, like a heartbeat. I don't even hear it unless I try to."

I listened for my heart and was comforted by the pounding of blood in my ears. I hadn't turned into glass after all. Phoebe was talking.

"I wonder what else you can do...astral projection? Passing through solid objects?"

"Do I have to feel like I'm behind a window the whole time?"

"You have to be in that particular space between air and light and dark."

That space made me feel nervous, like I wasn't all here, yet I was already missing the sound of the annoying silver note. I shook my head to rid myself of the memory of the sound, stomping my feet on the wet earth to assure myself that I was back in my own world. I was a little afraid of floating uncontrollably upwards, never able to attach myself to gravity again.

FREDERICO HAS GONE, LEAVING the tangled sheets on the bed. Carla carefully suspends a tiny woman from a strand of fishing line attached to the top of a box. Beneath the figure swaying in the air stands an angel, watching her.

We started for home. It was completely dark. I stepped carefully between the edge of the road and the ditch. Passing headlights blinded me for a moment in their examination before they swept over the hill behind us. I could hear voices from inside the cars, but whether they were talking to me or to each other, I couldn't tell unless they shouted, "Wanna ride, babe?" or "Get off the road, bitch." They disappeared in a hissing rush not unlike the sound of the wind that carried me into flight. My normal self would have flipped the bird to the more abusive drivers-by, but I was too preoccupied that evening. The memory of my flight was fading from me. What did it feel like? Why couldn't I hear the silver note now?

"I want to go back there and try it again," I said to Phoebe.

"You can fly anytime," she said. "You don't need to be standing in a patch of weeds to do it."

But trying to take off from the noisy, trash-strewn road's edge didn't seem right or possible.

"You do have to be in the right frame of mind," said Phoebe. "Would you please walk a little closer to the ditch? You're making me nervous."

We reached the sidewalk, and Phoebe breathed a sigh of relief. We were passing houses with lighted windows. It was a warm night; the windows were open and I could hear snatches of conversation and the clatter of dinner dishes being washed. The blue light of televisions illuminated living rooms where these contented people settled down on their couches to watch whatever was on. I was envious of their happy, dull little lives. They lived in cocoons illuminated by blue light. Like me, they knew what was going to happen the next day and the next and the one after that, but they could draw some comfort from it, knowing that the people they ate dinner with and watched television with would be with them through all those predictable days. I stopped suddenly. Phoebe bumped into me with a not quite imperceptible thud.

"You might warn me when you're going to come to a screeching halt. What are we stopping for?"

"Look," I said. A cat wandered in and out of the bushes in a front yard, hunting the chirping crickets. All the windows in the house were open, as though the people inside wanted to immerse themselves in as much spring air as possible before the dog days of summer hit and they would be sealed inside an air-conditioned box. I could see a man's head through the kitchen window. He was leaning over the sink, his shoulders moving. I couldn't see his hands. Another man walked past the windows of the living room, flipped on the television, and shouted into the kitchen, "Have you seen my shorts?" A tiny white dog yapped at us from inside its fence next to the house.

"They're not as happy as you think," said Phoebe.

"If they're not happy, they should be," I said. "Look at all they have."

"Certainly doesn't take much to satisfy you," said Phoebe. "A cat, a dog, a television, a kitchen sink, and you're all set."

"They know each other." I wanted to move in with those gay men in their happy cocoon of blue light.

I walked on. At the end of the block I turned right. After a few more blocks, Phoebe asked, "Isn't this the way to Beatrice's house?"

"It's a public sidewalk. I'm allowed to walk on it."

As we got closer to the white house where Beatrice stayed with her assortment of roommates, I imagined what I would say to her. Maybe something casual like, "Want to go out for a coffee?" I could see her look of surprise when I knocked on the door and she answered. No, that wasn't quite right. One of the roommates, probably the would-be poet, would answer, and she would call back into the house, "Beatrice! Somebody here to see you." The poet and I would wink at each other. The poet would know how much Beatrice had been missing me, though of course she would never have admitted it.

Beatrice would emerge from the back of the house. She would be wiping her hands on her jeans; it was her night to do the dishes. She would see me and stop in her tracks. On her face I would see all the passion and trouble of our year together. Then she would smile shyly at me and I would know that all was forgiven. All was forgiven.

We wouldn't say much to each other in the doorway, mainly because the poet would still be standing there. Beatrice would say to her, "I'll finish the dishes later, okay?"

The poet would nod and say, "Have a good time."

Off Beatrice and I would go, through the warm spring evening that promised everything. We might brush against each other by accident as we rounded a corner on our way to the coffeeshop. I would catch a whiff of the patchouli she always wore. Over coffee, even though I knew I was forgiven, I would say, "I'm sorry." Just for the record.

Beatrice would say, "It's all right, it's all right." She'd place her hand on my hand, right on top of the table, in a public restaurant. I wouldn't flinch or pull my hand away. Then she'd know she really could forgive me. After coffee, we would walk back to her rundown house, into her bedroom whose walls were covered with pictures she had cut from magazines and snatches of verse that the poet had written in calligraphy. She would throw the towel over the canaries' cage, and we would make love on tousled sheets under the wobbly ceiling fan. I would trace my hand along her back. Her skin was warmer at the base of her spine; cooler up toward the shoulders.

Phoebe said, "Isn't that Beatrice's house?"

I looked up with a start. It was smaller and dingier than I remembered, but I supposed the paint job was unlikely to improve with age. I stepped onto the creaking floorboards of the porch. My knees were stiff with nervousness. Only the torn screen door separated me from the inside. I rapped on the door. I rapped again and called, "Hello? Anybody home?" I could hear a conversation from the back of the house, perhaps from Beatrice's bedroom. I heard a strange woman laugh, and then I heard Beatrice's voice. I rapped harder. The voices fell silent. The stranger said, "There's someone at the door."

"Who the hell could it be?" That was Beatrice. I saw her shadowy form emerge from the bedroom. She was buttoning her pants. Her silhouette moved up the hall toward me.

"Yes?" She held her hand above her eyes.

"I was just passing by. I didn't mean to bother you."

"Alice! I couldn't tell who you were against the streetlight. Uh." She looked toward the back, toward where the other woman still was. "Come in, come in. How are you?"

I stood there all alone on the dark front porch. Over Beatrice's shoulder, I saw another form come down the hall. She put her hands on Beatrice's shoulders and peered at me.

"Is it someone I know?" she asked.

"This is my friend Alice," said Beatrice.

"Oh, right. Alice," the woman said.

"This is Felicia," Beatrice said.

I nodded at the little bitch. "I won't stay," I said. "I just dropped by to see how you were doing."

"I'm doing great," Beatrice said. "Are you okay?"

"Sure am," I said. "Work is going really well."

"I'm glad to hear it," said Beatrice. "It means so much to you. We haven't had supper yet. You want to join us?"

"No, thanks. I've got to get back home. There's someone waiting for me there," I said. I stepped off the porch as fast as I could. I waved at both of them. "Nice meeting you, Felicia." As I walked down the sidewalk toward home, I heard the screen door smack shut.

The inside of my condo was dark, which was not a big surprise since I hadn't turned on the lights before I left. The stuffy air smelled like some sort of plastic. I walked into every dark room and threw open the windows. I turned on the television. It blared at me. Its light didn't look at all blue. I turned it off. I sat down in the armchair in front of the silent television and lit a cigarette.

"Don't you want to turn on the lights?" asked Phoebe.

"No." My heart was breaking. All the sadness that I should have felt when Beatrice and I broke up washed over me. I heard myself sob and sob again in big gasping breaths. Someone stroked my hair.

"It'll be all right," Phoebe whispered. "It'll be all right." She stroked my hair the way my mother used to. I kept crying until my stomach hurt and I felt dizzy. My cigarette burned itself out in the ashtray. "Do you want to hear a story?" asked Phoebe.

"Sure," I mumbled. I rested my head against the back of the armchair and closed my eyes. Phoebe's voice came from somewhere above me.

WHEN BLANCHE GETS HOME, the hood of Ervin's truck is closed. A crumpled beer can lies next to one of the tires. She scoops up the can and tosses it into the dumpster next to the gravel driveway. It's just about dark. The blue light of the television flickers from inside the trailer out into the night. A few fireflies sparkle around the edge of their lot. Inside the trailer, it's noisy and close.

"Get the man to look at the backseat?" asks Ervin.

"Wasn't home," Blanche tells him. She settles down on the couch next to her husband. Ervin flips the TV channel every few seconds from the remote control in his hand. Flip. Noise. Flip. Noise. Blanche hears the kids squabbling in the back, but she doesn't go to investigate. They'll work it out.

"Bernard came by the shop today," Ervin says.

"Yeah?"

"After he left, one of the boys said he heard he was fooling around with some colored gal. I never will understand why a white man would want to mess with that trash."

"She's not trash."

"I don't know who or what she is, but it ain't right."

"No, it ain't right," agrees Blanche.

"Colored woman wanting to be white, that's what it is."

"Maybe it's Bernard wanting to be black."

"Bernard?" Ervin snorts. "No way, honey. He told his daughter she was no child of his if she ever went out with a black man. Said he'd come after her and kill them both."

"He said he'd kill his own child?"

"It's just talk."

"I can't imagine even saying a thing like that."

"Sure you can," Ervin laughs. "You told Joshua you were going to kill him just the other day."

"That ain't the same thing. I didn't mean it." Blanche lights a cigarette and throws the match into the ashtray that's on a stand next to the couch. "How long ago did Bernard say that?"

"Say what?" Ervin is flipping through the channels again.

"That thing about his daughter."

"I don't know. A while ago. Couple of years. She's married now."

"To a white man, I reckon."

"I reckon."

"You think it's true about Bernard and Shaquita?" asks Blanche.

"So you know about it too, huh? Nobody said what her name was today. I bet you even heard about it before me."

"I heard about it," says Blanche. "News gets around."

"It sure does in this place. I guess it's true. If everybody knows about it."

"That don't necessarily follow," says Blanche. "What I can't figure out is how a man that says he'd kill his own flesh and blood for going outside the race ups and does the very same thing."

"His ain't the only pecker with a mind of its own."

Blanche hoists herself from the sofa and goes down the hallway to change for bed. "Hey now," Ervin calls after her, "don't you ever let me catch you looking at a colored man."

"Okay, honey," says Blanche absently as she undoes her hairpins. She hears the buzz of the TV from the bedroom. In the mirror, instead of herself undressing, she tries to picture Bernard and Shaquita touching each other. Bernard probably stinks, he's so fat and sweaty. Blanche powders herself between her large breasts. She bets he weighs a ton, lying there on top of poor squished Shaquita.

What the hell do they talk about? Blanche doesn't think she's ever heard Shaquita say more than two words in a row. They must not talk. Just bump uglies. Blanche slips her nightgown over her head. She squeezes down the hall to open the back door and holler out at the kids. "Bedtime. Come on in."

They whine at her from the dark yard. "Now. I mean it." Blanche stands immobile in the doorway in her nightgown. The kids straggle in. Joshua tries to carry the puppy past her into the house. "The dog stays outside."

"He's lonely, Mama. Can't he sleep in my room?"

"No, sir. I won't have animals in the house."

She herds the kids down the hallway. Ervin's still in front of the TV. "'Night," Blanche calls to him.

"I'll be in shortly," Ervin says.

The next morning at work, Blanche's friend Donna nudges her as they punch their cards into the time clock. "Guess what I heard."

"What?" asks Blanche.

"Bernard's wife found out about Shaquita. She threw all his clothes out in the yard and told him to go find a bed in Niggertown."

"Did he go there?"

"You better ask Shaquita. She's the only one who knows."

"Leave Shaquita alone now."

"I wasn't going to say nothing to her," Donna says. "I'm just saying she'd be the only one who knows where Bernard went."

Shaquita's spot in front of her loom is empty. At break time, Blanche sits with the other women at the picnic table under the oak trees. It's damned hot. "Bernard didn't come to work," says Donna. "Have you seen Shaquita?"

"No, I ain't seen her," says Blanche.

"Whoooeeee," says one of the black women.

"Hey," Donna calls down to the end of the table where the black women are clustered, "any y'all seen Bernard out your way?"

The women laugh and shake their heads. "I ain't going near that mess," one of them says.

"They won't tell you nothin'," says Blanche. "They keep it to themselves if they know anything."

Shaquita is missing from her loom for the rest of the day. Blanche and Donna clock out together.

"Heard anything?" asks Donna.

"Not a thing."

"Shaquita ever show?"

"Nope."

"Damn this is good," says Donna, smirking. She follows Blanche out to the parking lot. Blanche walks faster to get away from her. "Wonder what the hell Bernard thinks he's doing."

"I don't know. I gotta take Joshua to the doctor," says Blanche. She slides quickly onto the seat of her car and slams the door closed.

"All right, then," says Donna, disappointed. "I'll see you tomorrow. Call me if you hear anything else."

Blanche stops by the grocery store on her way home. Joshua doesn't need to see a doctor. She pushes her empty cart through the cold air between cans of tomato sauce and boxes of spaghetti.

"He loves me." The whispered voice behind her startles Blanche. She whips around to see Shaquita holding a box of Pampers and a can of beans. She glances down at the Pampers.

"Oh, those are for my cousin," Shaquita says. "These beans are for Bernard. He don't have nothing to eat out in the woods."

"He's staying in the woods?"

"Yeah. Mama don't want him in her house neither."

Blanche thought of Bernard slipping like a pale ghost through the trees, watching and waiting in the pine forest outside Georgetown. His hands were folded in front of him as he peered through the underbrush.

"He says he loves you?"

"Uh-hunh," Shaquita nods. "I know it don't make sense. I believe him, though."

"Hmph," says Blanche.

"You would too if you heard him. He cries sometimes when he says it."

"I believe the both of you have taken leave of your senses."

"That's what Mama says."

"You listen to your mama. Bernard's got a family. You oughta be ashamed."

"I ain't ashamed."

"You love him?"

"I don't know." Shaquita looks away from her. "He's awful good to me."

"That's just the fastest way into your pants."

"No. That ain't it. Last night he told me he'd never touch me again if I didn't want him to, but he was determined to spend the rest of his life near me. Even if he had to stay in an old shack out in the woods."

Blanche shakes her head. "You all have made yourselves a big mess that you're gonna have to lie down in. What are you gonna do now? Get married and live happily ever after? What do you think your children are gonna do? They'll be neither white or black. Nobody's going to accept them."

"The folks in Georgetown will. There's all shades of folks in Georgetown."

"And what about Bernard's family? What about his wife? What'd she ever do to you?"

"Nothin'."

"Maybe she loves Bernard the way you don't."

"I didn't say I didn't love him."

"You never said you did."

Shaquita fiddles idly with the label of a can on the shelf. She starts to peel up a corner of it. "I might," she says.

The next morning, Blanche stands in front of her banging loom and thinks about Bernard and Shaquita in the pine woods. Down the line of looms, she can see Shaquita's head. Blanche feels jealous, but she isn't sure who of. Bernard is certainly no God's gift to women. Shaquita's just a little no-account colored girl who'll spend her whole life in the mill, just like Blanche.

Donna walks behind her and says in a low voice, "Look at her. Coming in here bold as brass."

"What do you want her to do? Quit her job?" Blanche flings back over her shoulder.

"Shameless," says Donna, shaking her head and walking down the line to her loom.

Shaquita leaves early. Bernard never does come into work. Neither of them comes back the next day, or the next.

A week later, Blanche pulls into the gravel driveway of the trailer park after work. She reaches into the mailbox and flips through the bills and circulars. There's a postcard of Chicago. She turns it over. The handwriting is long and flowing, just like a woman's, but it's Bernard's: *We run of to Shicago. No one to bother us her.* The little note at the bottom is Shaquita's: *I do so love him too.*

Blanche shakes her head. She sticks the card in the purse next to her on the front seat and drives to the trailer. She can hear the children squabbling. She scoops up the rest of the mail and brings it into the house, where she sets it on the table. Joshua and Brian and Shannon rush in and holler, "What'd you bring us, Ma?" They shuffle through the mail and pull out the circulars with glossy pictures.

That night, after the children have gone to bed, Blanche sits on the back deck. She smokes cigarette after cigarette. Ervin calls from inside the trailer, "You going to stay out there all night?"

Blanche slaps at a mosquito. She examines the bloody splotch it left on her arm. Owls back in the woods call to each other like barking dogs or banshees. "I'll be in in a minute. Just let me finish this cigarette." She stubs out her cigarette. The light comes on in the window of the master bedroom. After a little while, the light goes off. Blanche sits by herself and thinks about the secret love that might be all around her, or in the dark woods, where the owls are calling back and forth.

"It's all around me," I said, "but I can't touch it or feel it or even get close to it."

"Sounds like the way I feel," said Phoebe.

How long had it been since I had touched someone? This didn't count shaking the hand of the CEO as he passed by on his way out of the annual meeting, or muttering "Excuse me," as I brushed against someone in the lunch line. The personal space I had constructed was larger than most people's; it was definitely larger than anyone's who grew up outside North America. When writers visited from our subsidiary in New Delhi, we performed a circular dance around the room as they leaned toward me to get closer and I leaned back to get farther away.

"Starting with lust might not be a bad idea," said Phoebe.

"What?" I mumbled between sniffs. "The seven sins are in your plan, not mine."

"But you've got the virtues down pat; they're all you do. A little original sinning is what you need."

The lights of cars passing through the parking lot swept across the ceiling and walls of my dark apartment. They illuminated me sitting in my chair, but when they passed over Phoebe, she became fainter instead of more distinct. She glowed in the dark. In the white light she faded to a shadow of her self.

"Change is grace," said Phoebe. The next time a car's lights flashed through the window, not even the shadow of Phoebe could be seen. She had disappeared for the night, leaving me alone and unchanged.

CARLA LOOKS INTO THE BOX that holds the angel and the woman suspended in the air. Against one side of the box she has pasted a scene, cut from a magazine, of golden grasses waving under a blue sky. The sky on the back of the box is painted blue-black. Another figure of the same woman stands in front of a white house with yellow windows. What next? Carla wonders. What should go on the third wall of the box to make it whole?

I've always hated Sundays. They remind me I have no one but myself. Before I even get out of bed, Sunday morning washes over me and drowns me in despair.

On that Sunday morning, my apartment still smelled slightly of plastic despite all the open windows. As I brewed coffee, I made a mental note to buy myself something nice in the afternoon when the malls opened. I earned plenty of money; I might as well spend it. I tried to take good care of myself on Sundays.

I padded out to the sidewalk, coffee cup in hand, and picked up the heavy paper. I pulled out all the slick ads and tossed them into the dumpster on my way back inside. I settled down at the kitchen table, where I skipped the front section, flipped through the classifieds, and paused at the personals. Women Seeking Men, Men Seeking Women, Men Seeking Men, Women Seeking Women, and finally a category called Variations, although surely everything that could be sought had been already. I turned back to Women Seeking Women. Oh, good grief. Couldn't lesbians come up with anything better than walks on the beach, fireside chats, and dinner by candlelight? I turned back a couple more pages to the gay men's section, where the quality of the copy was generally higher. I mentally applauded the item where a guy was looking for a teenage boy "because I like the glow of braces in the dark."

If I wrote a personal ad, I would definitely improve on fireside-candlelight-beach. I picked up the gnawed pencil from the kitchen table and the envelope that held this month's electric bill. I turned the envelope over and poised my pencil over its blank surface. Which should I write—who I was or who I was looking for? Who was I looking for? I couldn't look for Beatrice anymore. Okay then, I would describe who I was.

For starters I wrote: *Attractive career-oriented woman seeks same.*

"Give me a break." Phoebe reappeared.

"Are you saying it's not true?" I challenged her.

"It's true, I suppose. It's also boring. What comes next? Something about fireplaces?"

I scratched out what I had written. Beneath it I wrote: *Lesbian with albatross seeks woman versed in seven sins.*

"Are you calling me an albatross?" Phoebe asked.

"If the shoe fits."

"Sounds like it ought to go under Variations, for the weirdos who are into birds."

I scribbled over that one, too. There wasn't any more room on the envelope. "Okay," I said as I pulled a pad of paper over to me, "here goes. Here's what I am." I wrote: *I am in the midst of change. Will you change with me?*

"Too vague," said Phoebe.

"How about this." I wrote: *GF who favors silk suits and haunts boardrooms seeks change. Will you come fly with me?*

"Don't ask them that!" said Phoebe.

"Don't worry," I said. "They'll think it's a metaphor."

"You're still just saying what you used to be," said Phoebe. "What will you be tomorrow?"

"Dunno," I said. My future was wide open that empty Sunday morning. For all I knew, I might move into a rundown house with a dozen other women and call myself a poet.

"I wonder what kind of ad Jo-Jo would compose," said Phoebe.

"I shudder to think." But my curiosity was piqued. I flipped the pad to a blank page and began to write.

ON A SUNLIT AFTERNOON WHEN he has nothing better to do, Jo-Jo strides down the long street to the photography studio that belongs to his friend Max. He sees Max's shadow moving behind the milky glass door before he turns the knob.

"Hi, guy," Max says.

Jo-Jo curls himself into a leather chair to watch Max work. Max is setting up for the next shoot. He does portraits, mostly in black and white. He adjusts the big lamps and positions three stools on the platform in front of his camera.

"Family group?" Jo-Jo asks.

"Of a sort. Three girls from around the corner. They've been living together for years. I haven't figured out who's sleeping with who."

"Un portrait de ménage à trois, eh?"

"Yeah, maybe they're all sleeping with each other."

"Or nobody. You know what dykes say about lesbian bed death."

Max says, "That's one thing I never will understand. I may be dead to the world in all other ways, but I can always manage to get it up."

"Braggy," says Jo-Jo.

"Ain't braggin' if it's the truth." Max bends down to adjust a wire. Jo-Jo admires the curve of his butt. He is a big white man who wears his hair in a brush cut.

"Gettin' a little broad in the beam, ain't you?"

"Shut the fuck up," snorts Max. "You're still looking."

"It's a whole lot to look at."

Max slings an empty film container in Jo-Jo's direction.

"Somebody's got to keep you in line, Miss Big Head," Jo-Jo laughs.

"If you'd like to be a help instead of a hindrance, why don't you go sit on that stool? One of the girls is about your height. I'd like to check out the angles before they get here."

Jo-Jo perches on the middle stool and beams at the camera while Max creeps around the perimeter of the platform adjusting things.

"You ever think about getting your portrait done?" Max asks.

"What would I wear?" muses Jo-Jo. "It'd be hard to narrow it down to just one outfit."

"How about doing somebody besides Judy Garland?"

"It's *not* Judy Garland."

"Whoever she is. The lady with big hair who sings 'Over the Rainbow.'"

"I played nun when I was a kid."

"Jo-Jo." Max stands with his hands on his hips. "That has got to be the strangest thing I have ever heard. Everybody else played doctor or cowboy; you played nun."

"You know," says Jo-Jo, "I would like to get my picture taken."

"You decided what to wear?"

"I'll let that be a surprise," says Jo-Jo.

The glass door opens and three women walk in. One of them is as tall as Jo-Jo.

"Hey, how you all doin'?" Jo-Jo smiles at them. "Be seeing you, Max," he calls as he leaves.

The next morning, Jo-Jo steps into the steaming shower and shaves himself from head to toe, even around his penis and balls, which takes some delicate work and nervousness, he can tell you. He does this every morning.

He stands naked and hairless as a long brown baby in his walk-in closet and considers. In front of the mirror, he holds a tie that a lover left behind in front of his bare chest. He has a little shopping to do.

It's been a while since he graced the portals of the men's department. Actually, not since he was a boy with his mother looking for a starched shirt just like the shirts of all the other boys. He heads for a rack of dark business suits. First, the very white shirt. Then a narrow tie with a hint of a pattern. This guy, whom he thinks of as Joseph, does not have a sense of style. Anything else? Ah, yes. Wingtips.

"I must view the whole ensemble," Jo-Jo says to the suspicious clerk as he lugs Joseph's wardrobe into the dressing room. He strips to his suede pants before he remembers. The socks. Businessmen wear those black stretchy things, don't they? He pokes his head out from behind the curtain of the dressing room. "Say, honey?" he calls to the clerk, a hunched-over white man who doesn't think Jo-Jo should be in his department at all. "Would you mind bringing me some socks?"

"What sort of socks did you have in mind. Sir?"

"The kind you're wearing. That'd be just fine."

A pair pokes itself through the curtain. "Here you are. Sir."

"Ooh. These are nasty." The limp socks appear to be some sort of nylon. They catch on Jo-Jo's nails.

"Will that be all?"

"For now, baby. But don't go too far away."

Jo-Jo dresses himself completely. The suit is charcoal grey with a barely discernible pinstripe running through it. He sees another man in the mirror. Joseph stares back, without a flicker of a sense of humor. "Man, you are a tightass," Jo-Jo whispers to him. "I am so glad I didn't turn into you."

"Is everything satisfactory?" the clerk calls from the other side of the curtain.

"Perfect."

"Will there be any alterations?"

The trousers are a little long; Jo-Jo can pin them. He wants to wear this getup out on the street. "Just give me some pins and a bag to put my other things in and I'll be on my way."

A plastic bag and a packet of pins are proffered through the curtain. "Thank you so much, darlin'."

Jo-Jo as Joseph strides up to the cash register and pays for his outfit in cash. "Do you sell briefcases?" he asks.

The clerk points toward the ceiling. "Just take the escalator, sir. They're directly over this department."

Half an hour later, Joseph leaves the store carrying a dark leather briefcase that holds the clothes of his girlish self. The heavy shoes make him feel like the lord of all he surveys. He nods to the car that waits to let him cross the street. A woman smiles up at him. He eyes his reflection in store windows and he adjusts his walk. No swish for Joseph. He tries lumbering, which seems to be the style that men like this choose. Aha. It's lunchtime and there are men dressed just like him all over the place. He walks behind one of them and watches him carefully. Hold the hips still and move the torso from side to side. Longer strides. This is so tiring. He slips up and relaxes into moving his hips. Stop that. By the time Jo-Jo makes it back to his apartment, his back is killing him and his face feels frozen.

There's one thing left to do. With the nail scissors, he cuts off every last one of his lovely nails and files them down to a conservative curve. "Ouch," he says as he closes the bathroom cabinet. The ends of his fingers run into the cabinet door.

Joseph is like a lot of men Jo-Jo has known for a night or an hour. A family man who says that his wife and children are the most important thing to him even as he devotes nights and weekends to his career. A man who bears the weight of the world. Jo-Jo straightens his shoulders. Joseph doesn't smile too much, unless he's enjoying the camaraderie of other men, men he drinks with, men he plays golf with. (A man like him doesn't necessarily smile when he's with Jo-Jo.) Jo-Jo applies a conservative mustache to his face: not too thin (don't want a pencil mustache like my grandfather); not too thick (don't want to look like a gay man). He wiggles his nose to make the mustache move.

The walk is still the hardest. He hasn't quite mastered it by the time he gets to Max's studio. He stands before the milky glass door and takes a deep breath. He raps on the glass.

"Door's open."

Jo-Jo stiffens himself and strides in.

"I WANT TO WEAR CLOTHES," said Phoebe.

"Try mine. I think we're the same size."

"Of course we are," she said.

Phoebe followed me to my closet. She reached over my shoulder and shuffled through the hangers. I had silk suits for work, flannel shirts and overalls for my summers in the mountains, even a couple of nightgowns that she skipped over.

"How about this?" She pointed to a grey silk suit hung with the cream-colored blouse I wore with it. Phoebe had good taste.

I pulled the suit and blouse from their hanger and laid them on the bed. "Um. You'll have to take off your nightgown." She blushed.

"I'll turn my back." I faced the wall. Behind me I heard the rustling of silk. Did angels wear underwear? Did I really want Phoebe to borrow mine?

"How do I look?"

I turned around. It was the opposite of dressing a dog, more like putting a paper bag over a flower. Phoebe's shining red hair made my snappiest suit look tawdry. The collar of the blouse was too big for her, or too small. She turned around and accidentally slipped her arm outside the material of the sleeve. "Whoops," she said. She shifted her arm back to where it was supposed to be, but each time she moved, part of her would escape from the suit. Phoebe and clothes did not exist on the same plane. She faded in and out in frustration, so that for brief intervals the suit danced around with no one in it. From the bed where she had tossed it, her nightgown glowed faintly.

"I would say you're not managerial material."

She glided to the mirror, the suit following slightly behind her. In the mirror, Phoebe's self was a disturbance in the light. The suit, however, was as real as I was. Its reflection hung empty in the space several inches above the rug. "You're going to scare people to death in that outfit," I said.

"Boo." She shook the arms of the suit in the air above her head. I wondered if ghosts and angels were the same thing. "No," said Phoebe. "Ghosts at least *used* to be real." She sat down heavily on the bed. I never knew angels cried.

"Why don't you put your nightgown back on?" I said. "You'll feel more like yourself." This time I peeked. Phoebe didn't have what one would call an anatomy. She was a glowing cylindrical cloud from neck to ankle. She slipped the nightgown over her head and floated around in front of me.

"It's no use," she said. She faded again, but only slightly. "And what's worse is I can't count on fading out either."

"You kept vaporizing while you were wearing my suit."

"That was different. *Then* I had a hard time staying visible, I was so upset. It's not as easy as it used to be to make myself disappear on purpose, or to stay visible on purpose." She scrunched up her face and turned invisible, although I could still catch the glow of her red hair. She popped back into view. "Today I just can't seem to stay gone."

It's close to midnight when Carla hears the *click-click-click* of Frederico's boot heels on the metal stairs on his way back from his rehearsal. He trips into the room, his walk a small dance. His black hair is tousled and damp. He sets his white motorcycle helmet on the table and grabs Carla to spin her around. Frederico is very strong for someone so small. They circle together across the bare wood floors to the edge of the bed. Carla disengages herself to sit on the futon.

"Dance for me," she says.

He takes off his boots first, then his jacket and shirt. He is clad in black leather pants. His white bare feet brush against the floorboards. In the silver moonlight and the silver streetlight that stream in through the enormous windows, Frederico dances.

The only sounds in the loft are his hard breathing and the squeak of his feet against the floorboards, but Carla thinks that she can hear the music he hears. He flings his head back until his spine is curved like a serpent's. He bows forward, twisting the serpent's coils. He spreads his arms like the wings of a heron. He writhes like smoke. He jumps across the room, his legs outstretched as though he could take flight if four walls and a ceiling didn't stand in his way. He lands and spins like a waterspout. He folds himself down onto the floor, slowly, slowly, until he comes to rest, panting, his arms bowed over his head.

Phoebe had more and more trouble making herself disappear. I'd never thought of our situation as "living together," but instead of a guardian angel I now had a ghostly roommate who paced around the apartment in a semivisible fashion. Mostly I only glimpsed her glowing red hair. Sometimes I could see the white of her nightgown. She shimmered in a dark corner of my bedroom while I slept. She was getting bored. Apparently staying on the human plane was not as interesting as flitting around on the angelic one. One night I was awakened by the dull mutter of the television in the living room and got up to investigate. Phoebe sprawled in the recliner in the flickering light with an expression of utter vacancy. I suggested she do some writing in these wee hours, but she said she was never in the mood then. "You can't just wait for inspiration to strike," I said.

"Why not? You do," she snapped back.

Make that a crabby ghostly roommate.

My moods weren't that great either. I couldn't seem to focus on the simple business of going to work and doing my job. Every morning, I left home later than the day before. I got up angry, poured my coffee in a rage, drove much too fast on the freeway when I finally made it out to my car, stormed down the corridor, and slammed my office door shut. I glared at the nicely clipped prison grounds. My skin felt cold. I cheerfully attributed this to early menopause, or the first warning signs of multiple sclerosis.

And my writers. Jesus, when had they turned into three-year-olds? Mary wanted a different office. She'd been in the same one for five years, what was her problem, but she was all grumpy because I'd given Bob, who had less seniority, one that was a tiny bit bigger. And his door probably had three hinges instead of two. Hinges are a status symbol where I work: the more hinges you have, the more important you are. I know my door has three hinges because I'm a manager, but I wouldn't know about anyone else's. I worked in tiny cubicles with no doors at all for years. Life could be worse, Mary.

I had never been particularly close with the other managers. There was too much at stake; keeping my own counsel was a matter of survival. An article in the newspaper about our company referred to the employees as "serfs." I secretly agreed. The other managers called a meeting and worked out a rebuttal letter to the editor. Brown-nosers. Serfs.

I sat in meeting after meeting. My job, it seemed, consisted of occupying space in conference rooms. An editor drummed her long fingernails on the table across from me. Had she lost her nail clippers? The *tickety-tickety-tic* made my skin crawl. I held myself back from strangling her. I pondered my friends and enemies list and had trouble recalling why some people were on one side and not the other.

Phoebe, too, was in a very uncomfortable place, neither fish nor fowl, angel nor human. She could taste food, but not eat it (she apparently didn't have a digestive tract yet). She was afraid to go outside where she could be seen. Sometimes she could pick things up, sometimes not. One evening, when we were sitting on the couch, she started to cry because she hadn't heard the silver note for almost fifteen minutes. She put her head on my shoulder and sobbed.

"What do you want, Phoebe?" I tried to pat her on the back, but my hand slipped into the cool translucence below the surface of what should have been her skin. This made me queasy; I drew my hand back and put it on my own more solid leg.

"Just because I wanted to write stories and touch things doesn't mean I wanted to lose everything else."

"Maybe you should go back to what you were."

"I don't know how." She sobbed. A drop of her tears fell on my hand. When I thought she wasn't looking, I tasted it. It was salty, just like my own. "I tried to fly the other day. I couldn't even get off the carpet."

"The room's too small."

"You know you don't need to run before takeoff. It's not like flying a kite."

"You're out of the habit."

She shook her head. "I can't go back."

I had no answer to comfort her. "It's getting late," I said. "I'm going to bed. I still have to work in the morning, unlike some people."

"Good night," Phoebe mumbled. She was staring bleakly into the middle distance when I left her.

PHOEBE WAS STILL SITTING ON the couch the next day. When Alice opened the door to go to work, Phoebe shivered.

"What was that?" Phoebe asked.

"You're cold," said Alice. "Put on a sweater."

"I can't," said Phoebe.

"Get up and move around. You'll feel warmer if you get some exercise." Alice was not a sympathetic person. She shut the door behind her, and once again Phoebe was left in the incredibly boring apartment with the same nasty beige wall-to-wall carpeting that had been there yesterday. Phoebe hoped Alice's life-change would result in better decorating choices.

She got up and peered out at the empty parking lot. Nobody was left in the row of condos except herself and a few mothers with squalling children. She watched a speedy baby scuttling down the sidewalk with the mother in hot pursuit. The baby looked up at her and waved. Phoebe hurriedly stepped back from the window. It was true that children could often see her, but did the baby see her because it was a baby, or could the mother see her too? She stepped gingerly back into full view. The mother was preoccupied with the child she had just captured, though, and didn't glance her way.

She went into the bathroom to look at herself. It was like peering into a badly lit two-way mirror. Alice's dentist used to have one of those when she was a kid. Alice made faces into it while the shadowy form of the secretary behind it ignored her. Phoebe could discern the outline of herself in the bathroom mirror, a transparent ghost with glowing red hair. She shut her eyes and tried to completely disappear. When she opened her eyes, the outline was still there, only a little fainter.

Then she would go in the other direction. She frowned and concentrated. A solid face appeared before her briefly, then dissolved. The silver note faded in and out; sometimes there was so much static she could barely hear it. She sighed. Alice's comb lay on the counter in front of the mirror. Phoebe picked it up and peered at it. It was dirty. What was it humans did with these things? She gingerly guided it through her hair and examined the glowing red strands pulled out in the comb's teeth. Would she grow more hairs to replace these?

She eyed the toilet. This was the chair where Alice liked to read magazines. It didn't look all that comfortable. Phoebe flushed it and watched the water swirl down the drain. Alice dropped something from her body into it. Phoebe wished she had taken more of an interest in human biology. It hadn't seemed relevant to her task. She dropped the comb into the toilet and flushed again. It got stuck in the drain at first, but with a few more flushes it was gone on its way to the sea.

She wandered into the bedroom. She wondered what Alice was doing now at that awful job she thought was so important. She ran her hand across the suits hanging in the closet. She could feel the differences between them. This was silk and that was wool. This was linen. She paused at the seersucker. Corporate Alice was quite the clotheshorse. The seersucker was both bumpy and smooth. Phoebe ran her hand slowly down the nubbled sleeve.

Oh, what to wear, what to wear. She yanked at a bureau drawer.

Her hand slipped off a couple of times before she got a good solid grip on the knob. Lesbian Alice wore nothing but jeans and T-shirts. They were crammed so tightly into the drawer that it wouldn't close all the way. Phoebe tugged at a wrinkled T-shirt, eventually extricating it from the tangle. She rooted around until her hand located a pair of jeans. She yanked at one leg and the jeans popped out, along with several other T-shirts that tumbled onto the floor. She held the pants up. There were gaping holes in both knees. She gingerly pulled her nightgown up and peered down to see if she had knees. She did, but they went in and out along with the rest of her. Sometimes there was only a glow that reached to the floor; sometimes it separated itself into legs and feet.

Gotta start somewhere, she thought. She pulled off her nightgown and threw it on the floor, where it flickered in and out of sight. She sat on the edge of the bed and tried to put the jeans on. It was like clothing fog: first she would be inside the pants leg, then outside of it. She cursed under her breath and glanced up, out of habit. She willed her vaporous legs to behave themselves and stood. She walked gingerly across the room. If she moved slowly enough, the pants could catch up with her. If she moved too fast, or forgot about having legs and glided, they lagged behind. Even when she stood still, wisps of herself escaped through the holes in the knees and hovered in front of her. Clearly, this would take practice.

She picked up the T-shirt and concentrated on molding her fluid self in the same shape. Two arms. A torso. A neck. She wriggled into it. She walked over to Alice's desk, her wings fluttering behind her like a shadow. She scanned the story of Jo-Jo's transformation. Metamorphosis was not a state available to angels. They were supposed to be the unchanging constants in a cosmos where even God had more than one form. But humans experienced so much through their bodies.

Change is grace, change is grace, she thought. *What did I mean by that?* If Alice could learn to fly, then surely she could learn to walk. Was it cold outside? How could she tell? What did Alice wear this morning? Some extra outer covering, she thought. She pulled a denim jacket from the closet and shrugged it on with difficulty. She paused before the bathroom mirror on her way out. She could pass.

A spring breeze ruffled the early green of the treetops and blew through Phoebe's red hair as she emerged from the building. She could tell the air smelled different. This was such a pleasant, peaceful morning, yet she saw no human beings out in the world enjoying it. People had so many feelings that seemed to get in their way, so many passions, so many curbs on their passion. The feelings Phoebe mostly had were curiosity, and wanting to create something on her own. Curiosity was what had gotten Eve into such trouble. Perhaps Eve was once an angel like herself.

Phoebe looked down at her own feet walking. She mostly stayed in contact with the ground. Heel, toe, heel, toe. Whoops. She'd forgotten about shoes. Was it too cold to be barefoot? She stepped through a puddle and looked back to see her footprints on the sidewalk. She turned around and saw someone coming toward her—a man with an Irish setter. Phoebe resisted the urge to disappear. She tried to smile graciously.

"Hi," the man said. "Nice day, isn't it?"

"Hi," said Phoebe, shyly.

The dog sniffed at her bare feet. "Looks like you're ready for spring," the man said.

"Yes, it is a nice day," said Phoebe. The Irish setter looked up into her eyes and winked.

"C'mon, Beau." The dog watched her over his shoulder as the man pulled him away.

When they had left, Phoebe began to tremble. She had never spoken to a human being who did not belong to her. The man didn't seem to find anything unusual except her bare feet. The dog knew exactly what was going on, but then she didn't expect to fool animals.

She looked down at her feet. They were feeling something and seemed a little bluish. This might be cold? She decided to put on shoes.

Phoebe paused at the apartment door. Alice always put something in the hole above the doorknob. A little shiny bit of metal. She looked around on the floor of the hallway for pieces of metal that might fit. She tried to walk through the door and was surprised by the solidity of it, of herself. Neither gave an inch. Was she starting to harden, like plaster? She grabbed the doorknob (she could grab!) and jiggled it, just like Alice did sometimes when the little metal thing didn't work. Never before had there been anywhere Phoebe couldn't go. Now she was Outside and she could not go Inside. There didn't used to be a difference between the two.

Very well, then, she would see the world without benefit of shoes.

WHEN I CAME HOME THAT evening, Phoebe was not sprawled on the couch. "Phoebe? You there?" I called. No response. I took this as a good sign. She must've relearned how to disappear. The place was a mess. As a human, Phoebe was a slob. A bag of potato chips had spilled out onto the coffee table. Another experiment in alimentation, I assumed. I popped a chip into my mouth on my way back to the bedroom. I caught a glimpse of myself in the bathroom mirror as I passed. Looked like hair trouble to me. I stopped to comb it. Now where was my comb? I could've sworn I'd left it in the bathroom this morning. I was getting as sloppy as my guardian angel.

I went into the bedroom with my hair still tousled. Half the bureau drawers were opened, T-shirts spilling out like potato chips. I grabbed a T-shirt for my evening wear and pushed the drawers almost closed with my knee. I had no doubt that Phoebe was watching me and chortling.

Every time I walked through the living room that evening, as I was making dinner and eating it and cleaning up, I expected to see Phoebe on the couch. The clock on the wall had a hollow tock I'd never noticed before.

After dinner, I turned off all the lights and watched TV. The blue light reminded me of something, maybe the light of heaven that Phoebe had talked about, or maybe the color of the sound that I caught a note of now and then. The sound came from somewhere up above me. If I listened too hard, it went away. I turned off the volume so I could hear the sound better. I made up stories to go along with the silent characters I watched. I ran my hand up and down my arm. My skin still felt different, not numb exactly, but glassy, smoother, cooler.

I woke up on the couch in a cold sweat in the middle of the night. I turned off the TV. A strange sort of silence filled the room. I listened. Phoebe. Phoebe wasn't there. It wasn't just that she had faded out, she really wasn't there. Not available to me. Gone. I felt naked and defenseless, and the room was much too quiet. I started hearing other noises, unnamed things coming to get me now that my protector was gone. This made no sense since I was pretty convinced Phoebe never actually did anything in the area of protection.

I searched for her in closets and behind chairs. I noticed Jo-Jo's story lying on my desk. Someone had added to it. Phoebe's handwriting was feathery, but legible.

YOU'VE COME DOWNTOWN TO have your portrait taken. While you wait for your appointment, you examine the pictures on the wall of the photographer's studio. There are all sorts of people in a line of pictures along the wall; the only thing the people have in common is that they're black.

First, there's the back of a nude man. His head is shaved. His arms are folded in front of him so that you can't see his hands. The curve of his silhouette looks like a seal, or some other molten creature. The muscles of his back glisten.

Next to him is a portrait of a nun. You don't remember enough of your Catholic schooling to recognize the order, but she's not one of these modern-day sisters that simply look like ordinary women with no style. This nun is the old-fashioned kind, with the edges of a starched white wimple pressing into her cheeks and forehead. The black of her habit is much darker than her skin. She looks inward; her expression is one of benign asceticism. You're a little envious of her transcendence.

Past the nun is a male dancer caught in mid-flight. His T-shirt is stretched across the broad muscles of his chest. He is reaching for something beyond the edge of the photograph.

Beyond him is a burly dyke who glares at you as though challenging you to a brass-knuckled brawl. Her rage flows out from the picture and washes over you.

The last of the portraits is of a man and a woman.

The photographer has come into the room to tell you that he's ready to take your picture now. He sees you examining the portrait.

"That looks like a nice couple," you say to him, just for something to say.

He smiles. There seems to be a joke. "Their name is Joseph," he says. "What do you really think of them?"

"Well," you pause for a moment, "if I were the husband in this photograph, I'd keep a sharp eye on the wife. She looks like trouble to me. She ought to tone down her hair and makeup, at least for the office Christmas party, if he brings her to that. And the gold tooth—really! She must be from the country."

The man stands behind his wife. He stares straight at the camera. He would look the same if he were before a firing squad or at a cocktail party. His shoulders are held back. His tie is dark, his shirt is white. His head is shaved. This is the only thing about him that distinguishes him from all the other businessmen you passed on your way here. Everything about him is neatly pressed. He's the kind of guy who wears ironed pajamas to bed at night. He stands with his hands behind his back. His white starched shirt matches the white of her dress. The whiteness shows up well against their dark skin.

The shaved head reminds you of something. You glance back at the nude portrait and see that the head has the same shape, only this view of it is from the front. You look at the blackness of the nun's skin. So that's what the photographer finds so amusing. They're of the same person—all of them, the nun, the dyke, the dancer, the wife.

The wife is seated in the foreground. She is dressed a bit over the top with a feather boa, big hair, and long, long eyelashes. A wide smile shows a gold tooth emblazoned with the initial *J*. She tilts a little toward the camera, as though inviting its embrace. Her hair swirls in black curls over her shoulders. Her dress is tight around the bodice before it flares out into reams of chiffon flowing across the floor like a static ocean.

I PORED OVER THE END OF Jo-Jo's story to see if Phoebe had left me any clues as to her whereabouts. What about Blanche? Would her story tell me something too? Blanche lived in eastern North Carolina. And

Carla? Carla was in Baltimore. Fortunately, Jo-Jo lived in some unnamed city that I could assume was my own for the sake of convenience.

A mockingbird was cranking up outside my window. It was getting light, which meant it was too late or too early to go down to the Cockpit, our local excuse for gay nightlife, and see if Phoebe was bellied up to the bar, chatting with Jo-Jo.

Today was Friday. I thought a minute. I picked up the phone. I held my nose as I left phonemail for my secretary. "Hello, Louise? This id Alice. I'b afraid I hab a code and won't be in today." I smiled to myself as I hung up the receiver. It'd been years since I'd done *that*. I had so much vacation saved up that I had gone beyond the maximum and lost days every year. But calling in sick was much more fun.

I couldn't find my favorite jeans with the holes in the knees, so I settled for a hole-less pair and, after a moment's pause, a T-shirt with a rainbow flag that Beatrice had given me and that I had never worn outside the apartment.

I knelt to peer under the bed in a last attempt to find the jeans with the holes. There was a glow in the far corner. My heart leapt into my throat. Phoebe? Had she been lying there the whole time? Was she sick? Could she be dead? I wriggled through the dust bunnies and reached out to the glow. It was Phoebe's nightgown, sans Phoebe. The nightgown shimmered and shifted and barely caught in my fingers. I pulled it back out with me. I was covered with dust, but the nightgown was not.

Phoebe shouldn't be walking around out there, wherever she was, without any clothes on. I packed a knapsack to take with me. Into it I put the nightgown, the legal pad with the stories we had written together, and, as I passed through the living room, the half-empty bag of potato chips, in case she was hungry when I found her.

It was just barely light when I stepped outside. It was a little cool, but I pulled the top down on my BMW convertible anyway. The air smelled fresh and new. I drove out of town fast, headed east, my teeth chattering.

I went past the field where I had learned to fly. It didn't look as though anything unusual had taken shape there. I was, for no obvious reason, completely happy. I think it had to do with the smell of the air, like crystal, as though crystal had a smell, or the empty ribbon of road, or the mist in low places over bridges.

How was Phoebe traveling if she couldn't fly? I saw someone with long red hair hitchhiking. I slowed down. The man with long red hair flipped me the bird when I sped up.

I came out of the rolling hills of the Piedmont onto the flat plains of eastern North Carolina. There wasn't much out there: fields of green soybean plants or brown dirt waiting for tobacco to be planted; shotgun shacks for the people who planted the tobacco; the enormous expanse of sky full of complicated clouds stirred up by the winds from the ocean two hours away. I stopped shivering as the sun rose and blinded me.

I pulled into a gas station. After I filled my tank, I walked into the store to pay. From the outside, it seemed like a tiny place, but inside it stretched into a pool hall and a snack bar that held bright red hot dogs lined up like little soldiers in their steaming glass case. A dusty bobcat snarled from the corner over the crackers. I peered through the darkness for any sign of life. "Hello?" I called.

I heard rustling in the back, but no one appeared. It was early yet. Perhaps the door had been left unlocked from last night. The white light of a beer sign glowed forlornly. I debated whether just to leave my money. Then I was chilled by the notion that the proprietor had been murdered and I was the first one on the scene. Gingerly, I leaned over the counter to see if there was a crumpled corpse lying beneath an open cash register drawer. The cash register was shut tight. There was no body in evidence. While I was hanging over the counter, I picked up a couple of packs of cigarettes from the shelf below.

I nosed around the rest of the store, the glassy eyes of the stuffed bobcat watching me.

"Hello?" I called again, weakly. To my relief, no one answered. The murderer must still be rifling the safe in the back. I poured myself a cup of coffee, blobbed some imitation creamer into it, and shook four packets of sugar before I poured them in and stirred. I like my coffee sweet and indigestible. I left the money on the counter, with a little extra because I didn't have exact change. As I pushed the door open on my way out to the car, the rustling grew louder. A big woman in a very tight sweater walked through the door from the back room. The rustling was the legs of her polyester pants rubbing against each other.

"Hey! How you?" she said. I jumped out of my skin.

"I left money for gas and coffee and the cigarettes," I said when I could get my breath back.

"That's all right, honey. You got an honest face." She smiled a smile full of perfect white teeth. She cheerfully rustled to the other side of the counter and popped open the cash register drawer. A pair of reading glasses hung on a sequined cord around her neck. "That right?" She put the glasses on. She looked at the money on the counter and then over her glasses at me.

"Yes," I said. I wasn't going to nitpick about the little bit extra.

"Thank you, honey," she said, and slammed the drawer shut.

"Have you seen someone with red hair wearing a nightgown pass through here?"

"I believe I'd remember a sight like that! Man or woman?"

"Woman," I said, since I had to choose one, and I didn't know any men named Phoebe.

"She kin to you?"

"Yes," I said. "She's my sister. She's lost."

"I'm real sorry to hear that, sugar. I'll keep an eye out for her." The woman's hair was swept in a brassy blonde mountain atop her head. "You can put up a notice if you'd like." She pointed to a bulletin board next to the door. On it were a few scattered squares of paper looking for lost bluetick hounds, or advertising ferrets, or cleaning in your home, reliable.

"Did she just get out of the hospital?" The woman was trying not to be too nosy, but the nightgown clearly had her intrigued.

"She was convalescing at home. She left while I was at work."

"I'm sure she'll show up soon. Don't you worry now." She handed me a stubby pencil and an index card on which to write my lost angel notice. How would I describe Phoebe without giving her away? No glow, no floating a few inches above the ground. She couldn't have been wearing the nightgown; I'd forgotten that it was in the backpack in my car. Unless she had a spare. I wrote: *Missing.* How tall was Phoebe if you subtracted the three inches of hover? It seemed we had always been the same height. I wrote: *5'5", red shoulder-length hair, blue eyes.* I couldn't remember what color Phoebe's eyes were, but blue seemed likely. *If seen, please call 776-8990.* I considered adding *Armed and Dangerous* just to infuse interest, but decided against it.

"You got a picture of her?" she asked. I shook my head. No picture of my sister. "We don't get too many hitchhikers on this road," she said. "It's a little off the beaten track."

I glanced casually at the business license tacked up on the wall behind the proprietor. "Blanche Mitchell," I read, and felt my face grow pale.

"You okay, honey?" Blanche asked. She put her warm hand over mine. She was not a ghost.

"Didn't you used to work at the mill?" I asked, tossing my line out wildly, hoping and not hoping for a bite.

"How in the world did you know that?"

I shrugged, caught. "Just a lucky guess. You looked familiar to me."

She peered at me, a little suspicious now. "I don't recall ever seeing you before."

I backtracked furiously. "I had a friend that worked at the mill. That's probably when I saw you."

"You don't say? What was her name?"

Here goes. "Shaquita. I forget her last name." Because I'd never written it.

"Shaquita! How in the world did you know her?"

Good question. How *would* I know someone who'd never been outside the county? "I used to have a job where I traveled a lot. I've been to the mill a time or two." Very vague, but perhaps it would do. It was new to be making up a story about myself.

Blanche didn't question that for the moment. "You hear anything from her?"

"No. She just disappeared. I never knew what happened to her." Best not to reveal anything more about what I knew.

"She moved to Chicago."

"Wow! That's a switch!" I was convincing enough to believe my own ignorance.

Blanche stared out the window at my car still parked at the gas pump. "I miss that gal," she said.

"When did you quit the mill?" I asked.

"They started laying people off a couple of years ago. Ain't that many jobs around here. I took over this place with what savings I had, but I don't know how long I can last. Not much business now that they've put in the new road to the beach."

I peeled the cellophane from a fresh pack and offered Blanche a cigarette. I lit hers and mine, and we smoked together in a little silence. I remembered how much I liked Blanche. "This is a nice place," I said, looking around.

"Used to be. I came here after school when I was a girl. Got Nehis and Cokes out of that cooler." She gestured toward a big red cooler in the corner, its white letters faded.

"Who shot the bobcat?"

"My husband Ervin. When he was young enough to stay up late enough to catch one. Thing gives me the creeps, but it's better than having it around the house." The bobcat's glass eyes stared past our heads. Blanche rustled over to the coffeemaker and poured herself a cup, black. "You look familiar," she said.

"Maybe you saw me around the mill."

"Maybe so."

"I have a face that looks familiar." This was true. I'm always being recognized by complete strangers. Perhaps I have more doubles than most. Blanche stubbed her cigarette out in the ashtray. "Help yourself to another one," I said. She nodded her thanks.

"Play a game of pool?" she asked.

"I'm not too good at it." Another lesson I'd missed in Lesbian School. That and softball, and disco dancing.

"You're bound to be bettern' me."

"Don't bet on it."

Blanche pulled a cue from the rack and sighted along its length to check for warp. Already she had the advantage. I picked up my cue and swiveled the blue chalk cube around its tip. This was the part I liked best. The chalk sifted in tiny blue flakes down the front of my shirt. I brushed it off onto my jeans and the floor. While I was happily preoccupied with the chalk business, Blanche racked the balls, sighted along her cue, and said "Orange, corner pocket." I'd forgotten about the part of the game where you actually had to predict what you were going to do. Miraculously, to me, the orange ball did exactly what she told it to. She popped a few more balls in, until finally one bounced gently and ineffectually against the felt edge.

"My turn?" I asked, hoping there was some rule I hadn't heard of that would prevent me from playing. Blanche nodded and blew smoke upwards in a bluish plume. I scrunched down in several locations around the table, peering at ball-level. Nothing looked good. I proclaimed, "Purple stripe," and pointed to a middle pocket. I drew my cue back and smacked the white ball off the table and onto the floor, where it rolled under the Bunny Bread shelf. As always, I was a minnow among pool sharks.

"Damn," said Blanche. Oh come on, surely she'd seen someone do *that* before.

"Don't tell me you learned how to play when you were a little girl drinking Nehis."

"I was too short then. Me and Ervin used to play pool when we were dating." Blanche laughed. "Ervin was just about too short to see over the table."

I looked up from where I was rescuing my ball from under the Bunny Bread. Blanche's smile was a little sad. "He passed a year ago."

"I'm sorry to hear that."

"Only forty-two. Had a bad heart nobody knew about. You'd think anybody'd have a heart attack it'd be me instead of skinny old Ervin."

I rolled the dusty white ball back onto the table. "You got any kids?"

Blanche nodded. "My girl Shannon's old enough to take care of the two boys. Not that they mind her."

We finished our game of pool, and I managed not to lose any more balls under the Bunny Bread. I drank the dregs of my cold coffee and tossed the cup in the trash. "You take care of yourself, Blanche," I said.

"You, too, honey. Hope your sister shows up soon."

"Thanks." The screen door slammed behind me. I continued on my way to find Phoebe.

The sun climbed up the sky as I drove along the back roads of the coastal plain. Seeing Blanche made me think that Phoebe might be around here somewhere. My nose was getting sunburned. I hadn't looked at the map of North Carolina that lay folded in my glove compartment. I followed the principle of sinistration: make a left turn whenever possible. This technique led me past cypresses growing in pale green swamps, Spanish moss hanging from their branches. For a while, a channel of quiet black water ran next to the road. Clusters of turtles basked on logs jutting out in the spring sun. As each radio station faded away, I tuned into another.

I imagined going home to a little sharecropper's cabin like the ones I saw in the fields. There would be an old woodstove, a table, a chair, a cot. That would be all. I would eat a simple meal every evening, maybe pinto beans and cornbread, and I would sleep beneath a cracked glass window in the light of the full moon. I forgot who I was and became just a woman traveling. I didn't have a name. The road is a good place to reinvent yourself.

All that day I drove on highways that used to be important before the interstate was built, highways interrupted by railroad tracks in the middle of hot, dusty towns. In these towns, people ate their lunch in a restaurant on the corner by the main traffic light. What would it be like to have a lover in every little place I passed through? They would be waitresses, mill workers, tobacco pickers. They would spit and cuss and be glad as all get out to see me. We would have quick sex before I went on up the road.

I passed a woman waiting to cross on her way to a restaurant by the railroad tracks. She was wearing a cheap purple dress that was too tight across her hips. She stood with the grace of a statue, solid from her work in the mill or the tobacco fields or having too many children to look after. Her skin was dark brown against the bright lavender of her dress. I thought about going with her into her trailer, closing the bedroom door against the babies, and feeling the sweat on each other's skin. In my rearview mirror I watched her slowly walk across the road.

A few miles later, I pulled off the highway into a Hardee's. A tough-looking woman was sitting in the corner. Her hair was straight and black and greasy. It had streaks of grey.

She stared ahead of her, slowly eating her fried chicken, bite by bite. It was three o'clock in the afternoon; working people were in offices or mills or out in the fields. I liked being a stranger. I could think anything I wanted to about anyone I saw and believe it was true. The tough woman in the corner ran a bootleg house on a back street. She was up all night selling shine to the neighbors; she slept most of the day before she got up to eat fried chicken at Hardee's. She'd done time for her illegal hootch-selling. Now she knew enough to pay off the sheriff's boys and they left her alone. I ate my french fries, one by one, and watched her. She left chicken wrappers strewn all over her table and walked heavily out the door.

I drove for so long I started to see shapes out of the corner of my eye, figures that could have been Phoebe or my lost twin or nothing at all. I pulled up to a string of cabins that had a flickering VACANCY sign in front. My room was dark, with a window that overlooked the swamp out back. The cable TV only got three stations. I watched all three for five minutes and turned it off. I flopped down on the sprung bed and stared at the fly-specked ceiling. If I closed my eyes, I could still see the road stretching before me and feel the jostling of the car over asphalt. I got up from the bed and pulled the legal pad out of the backpack. I found a pen and lay on my stomach to write some more of Blanche's story. The high sound of tree frogs came in through the open window.

ERVIN COMES TO BLANCHE IN A dream one night. His skinny self presses against her; he creeps up the length of her body. He makes love to her the way he never did when he was alive. "Remember this," he whispers before he slips away and she awakes to another day in the trailer.

She glances up at the clock at the head of her empty bed. Almost five. Time to get up and fix lunches for the kids and leave a note for Shannon and go over to the gas station. Blanche has beaten the sun out of bed since she was ten years old and pulling tobacco. She pads down the dark hallway past the bedrooms where her children sleep. Ervin's sweat-stained baseball cap still hangs on a hook by the back door. She hasn't had the heart to take it down, even though she's gotten rid of the rest of his clothes. His truck is parked out front. Probably won't start anymore. Blanche keeps the hat by the door because she can't remember all that much about Ervin. The whole family had their pictures taken at Sears six months before he died. It doesn't really look like them. They are all dressed up, for one thing. Their smiles are for the camera. Shannon and Joshua and Brian all sit much closer together than they ever would outside of a picture. They are some other family who never fights and never drinks and goes to church on Sundays. She'd like to have a picture of Ervin the way he was, sitting at the kitchen table, a can of beer at his elbow, untangling line from his reel.

She turns on all the lights and the pump at the gas station. She checks the shelves and reminds herself to call the bread man and the oil dealer. She can still feel Ervin's touch on her skin.

A low-lying mist clings to the road out front. A figure walks out of the fog toward her store. A little man, like Ervin, only black. He touches his cap when he comes in. "Mornin'," he says.

Blanche nods, suspicious. She's here all by herself.

"I ran out of gas. Can I trouble you for a can? I'll bring it right back." He smiles.

"Five-dollar deposit," says Blanche.

"Five dollars is all I have. How'm I going to get the gas too? I ain't going to steal your can, I swear. I stay just down the road."

"Got a driver's license?" asks Blanche. "You can leave that with me."

"Sure do." He hands her the plastic card. She lifts the red metal can over the counter to him. He gives her a five-dollar bill. "I'll pick up the change when I come back."

She watches him fill the can and lug it into the mist to his stalled car. The light of the sun is just brushing the tops of the trees. She picks up his license and reads it. "Ardis Alston." It isn't a good picture. He looks better in real life. He's forty-five, a little older than Ervin when he died. You can never tell the age of those people by looking at them. Doesn't wear corrective lenses. He does live just down the road, if he hasn't moved since the last time he took the driver's test. She hears the rumble of an engine behind her. She looks out the window. Ardis is driving a big tan Oldsmobile with the muffler dragging on the ground. It'd been halfway painted grey before somebody changed their mind. That car needs a lot more than gas.

"Here's your change," Blanche says when he walks in. "You think your car's going to make it much farther?"

Ardis laughs. "If it make it to my next paycheck, I'll be satisfied." He glances at the change on the counter. "I'll have a cup of coffee, too." He pours himself an enormous cup. Blanche subtracts the amount from the change left and hands it to him. His fingers feel like leather where they brush against hers. "You have a good day now," Ardis says. The screen door smacks shut behind him, and the little bell tinkles. He pulls out onto the road, the muffler throwing sparks as it clatters along the pavement. He has a brake light missing. Blanche sits back on her stool behind the counter and waits for the next customer.

I AWOKE IN THE MORNING with my face crumpled against Blanche's story. I got on the road again just as soon as I could. I needed to keep moving, to keep looking for Phoebe. Maybe she could explain why our stories were coming to life.

14

I kept driving, my hair stiff from the dust blown into it. Behind the noise of the wind and the radio, I heard snatches of another note, or maybe it was the hum of my tires. I rubbed my arm. My skin must be getting numb from the constant blast of air. The sun rose higher in the sky. I bought brunch at a different Hardee's. With the greasy bag next to me on the seat, I turned down a dirt road that meandered through enormous ancient trees and then a grassy field. I pulled over and reached into the bag to hunt around for my orange juice and biscuit.

The grasses fluttered in the breezes. It was a day in late spring when you could convince yourself that summer would be bearable after all because here it was a perfectly warm day and this wasn't so bad. A day not too long before the sky turned white and the air grew thick, before the three months you spent being drenched with sweat the whole time you weren't freezing in front of an air conditioner.

I perched on a stump at the edge of the field and ate my biscuit. I hadn't tried to fly since that day in another field with Phoebe. Groups of clouds tangled and untangled themselves in the stronger winds in the blue sky up above me. I supposed angels weren't blown around in the wind like birds. I finished my brunch. I lay down on a fairly dry patch of grass next to the stump and watched a bird high, high up—maybe a seagull or a hawk—float above me on the air currents.

I could hear the note more clearly now, not that I really wanted to. Reluctantly, I rose to my feet. I kicked off my sandals. The note grew louder. Without even trying, I rose straight up from the ground, between the wind and the light somewhere, the note pulling me upward. I decided not to be afraid this time, even though I had no guardian angel to protect me from all the things I did not know.

As I rose high enough to see the rectangle of field spread out below me, I could hear a fluttering. I glimpsed something white on the edge of my vision and spun around; I could have sworn it was a nightgown, or the feathered edge of a wing. I tried it again, giving myself more velocity this time. Again and again, until I was whirling like a top high above the woods and swamps. Whee! As I spun, I could hear the fluttering more. A chimney swift whizzed past me, and I could feel the breath of its flight. I halted myself and spun just as rapidly in the opposite direction. I wasn't getting dizzy, only giddy. The sense that there were thousands of wings near me grew until I could see, just barely, their white forms flapping and the shadowy shapes of the angels they belonged to. They were all around me, as if we were a flock of migrating swallows, a mass of us cavorting above the earth. I couldn't make out the angels' faces, but I could see they were merely playing in the upper air, spinning and swooping (I'd have to try that). It seemed to me that they were laughing.

An angel brushed past and I reached out to touch it. A pause of cool glassiness before it moved beyond my grasp. Phoebe? Was Phoebe up here? Would I be able to pick Phoebe out in a crowd of others like herself? The ghostly angels surrounded me in a circle and danced. I tried swooping and succeeded in hurtling at the earth at high speed until I brought myself to a screeching halt inches above the ground. Slowly I rose again. Was that faint applause I heard from the circle of dancers high above me? As I ascended, I looked toward the faraway coast to see if I could glimpse the sea. Something else caught my eye: another figure in flight, only it wasn't an angel or a chimney swift. It was a person, like me, slowly rising up toward the sound of the silver note. Tentatively, I waved. He or she waved back. It was too far away to discern gender or age. Were either of us visible to a mere mortal standing on the ground? I looked down and spotted a little kid on a bicycle far below. He was watching something in the sky around me, but was it only the dance of the swifts he saw?

I had no wings, yet I was flying just as well, or would be with a little practice, as the angels around me. The wings must be for decoration, or they must be what I expected an angel to wear. I reckoned that maybe angels looked different to different people, depending on your expectations. Who knew what a Hopi would see, or someone living in the fourteenth century when the wings of angels came in all sorts of colors.

I never was scared, suspended above the earth with no visible means of support. I floated gently back down to the ground and landed on my feet, as though I had been standing all along. I could see the dark figure of the other human remaining high above me. I felt as though I hovered three inches above the dirt, although when I looked down at my feet, they were firmly ensconced in my sandals. These were solidly on the ground, enough to make a slight indentation in the soft earth.

"Oh, I have slipped the surly bonds of earth," I whispered to myself. It did not seem strange to me that my life had become unbelievable. I reached for my car door and had trouble grasping the handle. From that day on, the high note that Phoebe heard would always be there. I only noticed it when I listened for it.

I drove down the dirt road with angels swirling in the dust clouds that rose up behind and above me.

THIS MORNING, WHILE FREDERICO sleeps in her big bed, Carla is working on several complicated boxes that are related to each other, although she's not sure how just yet. In one, she's put the big blonde doll and a little dark one. There's also furniture in the box: a flat table from a dollhouse that she's covered with green felt to make it look like a pool table, a tiny cash register from a supermarket set for children, some miniature cans and plastic loaves of bread from the same set. The two figures inadvertently lean against each other because Carla hasn't decided what to do with them yet.

Another box holds white cotton puffs with tiny figures stuck into them. Most of the figures have white cardboard wings, but two, who look just alike, do not. The two figures are on opposite sides of the box. They can probably see each other through the cotton puff clouds.

The third box is the most interesting, she thinks. Another winged figure is seated on a bar stool in front of a cardboard bar not unlike the one where Carla works every evening. The walls of the bar are pink. The angel's wings are made of lighter paper than cardboard; they're looking bedraggled. Carla glues a cotton puff on the wall above the winged figure's head to indicate smoke. A wingless figure dressed in motorcycle garb is seated next to the winged one. The plastic boots of the motorcycle rider are curled around the legs of the barstool.

I MISSED HAVING SOMEONE like Phoebe to share my adventures with. I wanted to find her to tell her what I'd been up to while she was disappeared. Who else would understand my story of flight and swallows? The dirt road ended on a paved highway. I turned left again. At some point, surely, I'd have to end up where I began, but so far nothing was looking familiar. I slowed down to read a brown metal sign: JAPONICA-SMITH PLANTATION 5 MILES. Strange name for a plantation. Perhaps this would be different from the usual Massas and Mammies remembrances of the good ole days Before the War. I didn't really expect Phoebe to be sightseeing, but I wasn't having any luck spotting her in my wanderings. Japonica-Smith was probably just as promising a place to stop as anywhere else.

As it was, I drove right by the last brown sign and the turnoff for the plantation. I retraced my route and bumped over railroad tracks to follow a winding road that ended at a stone wall. The iron gate across the entrance was open. I drove slowly beneath enormous magnolias whose lemon scent clouded the air. I was about to decide that this would indeed be the same depiction of the happy South, when I began passing between lines of broken and bizarre figures on both sides of the road: Oriental wise men whose cement features were melting together, ceramic camels missing a leg or two, turbaned genies with paint peeling from their dark faces. They watched me as I drove up to the parking lot in front of the gift shop.

The fee to enter Japonica-Smith was an exorbitant ten dollars. "It's very interesting, very unique," the woman in the gift shop assured me, with just the hint of a smirk. I gathered she meant *unique* as in *bad*. Outside the shop, the fluffy white clouds I was flying in a couple of hours ago had assembled themselves into real weather and it had started to rain. I wondered where angels went when it rained. My ten dollars would keep me dry for part of the day if Japonica-Smith's roof didn't leak. "The next tour of the house starts in half an hour," the woman said as she handed me my ticket. Since I was the only visitor in evidence, it didn't look as though timed tours were a necessary crowd control measure. "Feel free to explore the grounds while you're waiting." Well, it wasn't raining that hard. I stepped out of the other side of the gift shop, past a 1950s vintage Cadillac, and walked onto a cement path that led through the woods in the direction of the main house. The leaves of the understory quivered as the raindrops fell on them.

There were more statues scattered among the trees in the same decaying condition as those along the road: battered elephants, noseless Indians. Their arrangement seemed random, as though they had wandered into the forest all by themselves before freezing in place. I came into a clearing and saw an enormous two-story red pagoda. There was a collection of murky green pools in front of it. I could barely make out the occasional shifting scarlet shape of a koi beneath the layer of algae. Cement stepping stones connected one pool with the next. I amused myself by tiptoeing on top of them as the koi slipped beneath my feet. A green knee-high pagoda decorated the edge of one of the pools opposite the enormous red one.

The place seemed ageless: too new to be ante bellum, yet very old in its decadence and sense of loss. It was an empty place, odd for a Saturday in spring when there should have been hordes of disappointed tourists standing around in the rain.

I peered into the first story of the red pagoda. The floors were bare cement. In one corner was a stack of tattered wicker chairs. Parties were held here a long, long time ago. Japonica-Smith was starting to depress me. I climbed the stairs around to the back of the pagoda where there was a half-empty swimming pool. The leaves of last fall floated on the surface of the water. Beyond the swimming pool stood the mansion itself, a long, rambling mass of dark brick that went on and on in wing after convoluted wing. No other sightseers were huddled on the front step waiting for the beginning of the next guided tour.

I slogged across the yard as the rain became more insistent. Through the front door screen, I could see a shape moving. As I drew closer, the door opened and a slender young man with a ponytail beckoned me inside. "Come on in out of the rain. The next tour starts in five minutes." He was extraordinarily enthusiastic for someone who had only a single paying customer. "May I see your ticket, please?" And extraordinarily vigilant about preventing free rides. One would have thought he'd have been desperate for any company, ticketed or not.

We stood in silence in the dark foyer while he consulted his watch every minute or so. At last, he made a show of leaning out the door again to make sure no one was hurrying across the lawn to join us, faced me, and commenced his tour.

Our first stop was the bathroom off the foyer, which he described in excruciating detail. I admired that. "When was this house built?" I asked. The young man looked annoyed at my interruption of his patter. "Japonica-Smith was built in 1920." We moved on into a grand hallway with portraits of the owners and much discussion by my guide of the wood paneling and the chandelier that hung above us. The portraits faced each other across the hallway; they both looked solid and grey. "Are the owners still alive?" I interrupted again. "I was just about to get to that," he snapped. "Mr. Smith died in 1937. Mrs. Smith died in 1958."

I gave up asking him questions and turned my attention to the bric-a-brac that covered every flat surface: animals and people and chimeras. The Smiths, for whom Japonica-Smith was named, were collectors and Orientalists. They wandered Asia scooping up every object they could lay their hands on. We moved through the hall into an enormous room two stories high. Tapestries hung on the stone walls. The pipes of an organ took up one end of the room. And, of course, there were more statues. Empty as the house was of human inhabitants, it was crowded with these diminutive beings, watching us and waiting, and probably getting up and dancing about as soon as the doors were locked for the day and the lights turned out.

My guide and I snaked our way along a narrow twisting stairway up to the bedrooms, which had also seen better days. Torn satin coverlets were draped over the beds. "Each room has its own theme," he said as we entered the French Provincial. The statues there had a slightly less Asian cast. On the bedstand stood a winged figure that looked familiar. I leaned over the velvet rope separating me from the interior of the room.

"Please don't touch anything," he fussed.

"May I look at it more closely? I promise not to touch it."

He debated with himself, then glanced around cautiously as though the palace guard were waiting in the wings to apprehend both him and me at the first sign of miscreancy. He unsnapped the velvet rope and stood back to let me pass. I kept my hands carefully folded behind my back, in his full view, as I bent over the marble angel on the table. It was Phoebe. It was her face, her wings, her hair, her truculent expression. She even had her arms folded the way she did when she had had just about enough of me. The guide cleared his throat. My time in the inner sanctum must be running out.

"Do you know anything about this angel?"

"No. This was where Mrs. Smith slept after Mr. Smith passed away."

The origin of the angel was not a part of his prepared speech. Phoebe had made only glancing references to the people she had accompanied in the past. She'd never mentioned heiresses or mansions full of funny statues.

"Thanks." I smiled at my keeper as I walked back to the doorway.

"No trouble at all," he said tersely. He clicked the velvet rope closed behind me. I followed him down a dark corridor, listening for the sound of someone else. If Phoebe had indeed stayed here in the life before me, it was not unlikely that she would return to her old stomping grounds. She who had lived in the world so long, yet remained so unfamiliar with it, might need to find a spot that felt like home to her. I heard a scratching on the other side of the paneled wall.

"Mice," said the young man.

Or angels, caught between past and present, here and there. We wound our way down an unlit stair on the opposite side from the one we had climbed. "That concludes our tour," the young man said. "Please feel free to explore the gardens. Mr. Smith's heart is buried under the stone monument you can see from this window."

"His what?"

My guide smiled slightly. Making his charges jump was no doubt his favorite part of the tour.

"His heart. In his will, he requested that his heart be buried here, at Japonica-Smith."

"What about the rest of him?"

"They flew over the grounds and scattered his ashes from the plane."

"Sounds like a very literal interpretation of the will." And an unnecessary amount of dissection.

"It's what he wanted." The young man showed me out a different entrance, one that opened onto the broad expanse of lawn at the back of the house. The rain had let up. Through the window of the house, I saw him settle down in a folding chair with a newspaper to wait for the next crowd of visitors. I didn't see any angels fluttering over the green grass, but I did spot someone on the other side of the boxwood that lined the walkway to Mr. Smith's heart. I could see the top of her head, and where the boxwood thinned, the rest of her. It was a woman with wildly curly black hair that stood out like a halo, walking back to the house. She wore a camera slung around her neck. When I got to the end of the walkway, I looked back to see the woman standing at the opposite end, watching me. As soon as she saw I saw her, she spun on her heel and walked away. I turned back to study the inscription on the gravestone: PLUCK OUT THE HEART OF MY MYSTERY.

Frederico is at rehearsal. Opening night for his troupe's performance is next week. If Carla were looking at the window instead of the
box that she's working on, she'd see her own reflection in the dark
glass, a rippled form bending over the table with great concentration.
The apartment has gotten more crowded with half-finished boxes;
the story of each box has expanded beyond its own walls. Box after
box continues the same story in installments. Carla is working on the
boxes that hold the angel.

The figure with tattered paper wings staggers out of a bar in the
company of the motorcycle rider. The sign over the door reads GAYLA
TAVERN. The two are hanging onto each other. It's hard to tell who is
supporting whom. Carla has a tiny paintbrush that she uses to paint
expressions on her people. The expression on the winged figure can
only be described as one of curiosity, as though she is wondering
what will happen next. The motorcycle rider is just working on
remaining upright and putting one foot in front of the other. His
companion will probably learn more about drunkenness than lust
tonight.

The box next to this one is also under construction. It looks like the morning after the bar of the night before. The motorcycle rider is buried under a pile of blankets on a motel bed. His eyes are shut; he's fast asleep. The figure with the tattered wings is searching through the pockets of his jeans that are slung over the back of a chair in the far corner of the room. She's pulled a key ring halfway out of one pocket. Before he fell into bed last night, the motorcycle rider kicked his boots off. They're by the end of the bed, their soles firmly planted on the floor, their leather calves folded down. The rider's round black helmet sits atop the dresser by the chair. Carla has made a replica of Frederico's helmet out of plastic clay.

The next box takes place outside. Puffy white clouds of cotton are stuck against a blue sky. A long grey band of road bisects the bottom of the box; the band itself is split by a double yellow line. Stands of tall trees lean over it from both sides. Down the grey band a Harley flies, its rider's long red hair fluttering out below the edge of the helmet. The sleeves of the black leather jacket she is wearing almost cover her hands. On her feet are boots that are much too big. Inside the helmet you can just make out the broad smile painted on her face. There's only one tattered wing affixed to her back now. The other wing has drifted to the edge of the road, torn off by the wind.

Carla sets the three boxes down on the floor at the edge of the room and picks up another box from under the table. It's the one that holds the big doll and the little dark figure leaning against each other.

ALL OF BLANCHE'S DAYS ARE pretty much the same. She gets up as soon as the alarm buzzes in the dark, pulls on slacks and a blouse, sets out milk and cereal for the kids, and drives down the empty highway to her store. She opens it at 6:00 A.M. to take advantage of construction workers stopping by for breakfast on their way to their jobs. Depending on the season, sometimes she gets a crowd right when she opens up. In late summer the tobacco pullers are waiting in her parking lot for coffee when she arrives. There's hunters in the fall. She can hear gunfire in the woods back of the place through January. Now, at the end of spring, not much is going on except the occasional lost tourist trying to get back on the interstate. The locals stop for gas if they can't make it into town where the prices are lower.

On this particular morning, which is after the morning that strange woman came by looking for somebody she claimed was her sister, and after the morning the colored man said he ran out of gas, the parking lot is empty. Blanche has gotten so she likes her mornings by herself, away from the kids, even though her solitude is bad for business. She's just settled down with the paper and her coffee and cigarette when she hears gravel scrunch under tires in the parking lot behind her. She turns in irritation to look out the window. A big Oldsmobile, half grey, has pulled up to the door. The door on the driver's side pops and groans as Ardis opens it. Blanche turns her back to him before she can see him wave. What's he doing here again? Ardis comes in, the bell on the screen door tinkling his arrival.

"Can't you keep gas in that car?" asks Blanche.

"Don't need gas today. Just stopped by for coffee."

He goes over to the coffeemaker to pour himself a cup.

"That's good coffee," says Ardis. This isn't true. It's cheap and it's been sitting in the pot since yesterday. What does he want? Blanche doesn't say anything, just sips from her own cup. He's still standing around. He must not have to be at work soon. "Where you stay at?" he asks her.

"Not too far from here." She resists glancing down at the pistol she keeps under the counter.

Ardis wanders around examining the merchandise and sipping his coffee. He tosses his styrofoam cup into the trash. "Well, then." He slaps a few coins down on the counter and makes her jump. "I'll be going. You have a good day now."

Blanche scoops up the change and tosses it into the cash register drawer as the bell tinkles on his way out. She doesn't care if he never comes back.

The next morning, Blanche is running late and by the time she gets to the store, Ardis' car is in the parking lot, the exhaust rumbling white out of the tailpipe in the early morning chill. She considers driving on by and going to the police station in town to report him, except he hasn't done anything but buy coffee and gas from her and stay long enough to make her nervous. Another car pulls in behind her, somebody else wanting gas. Blanche gets out and unlocks the door of the store. Ardis follows her in. The other driver waits at the pump. She turns it on and waves okay at him through the window.

"Coffeepot's empty," she tells Ardis.

"I don't mind making it," he says. The other customer is on his way in, so Blanche just tells him, "It's on the shelf underneath the pot." He slips the packet of coffee into the filter and pours the water like he does it all the time. The other customer pays for his gas and leaves. Ardis stands around waiting for the coffee to finish dribbling into the glass pot.

"You on your way to work?" asks Blanche.

"My next job. I been delivering papers since two. I load trucks and clean up over at the feed mill. This coffee's what keeps me going. Glad you're open so early. Pour you a cup?"

"Okay," says Blanche.

He hands her a cup and then glances at his watch. "I best be going." He digs in his pocket for change. Blanche waves him off. "You don't need to pay. It's free if you have to make it yourself."

Ardis nods his thanks. His car rumbles out of the lot and Blanche is left alone with her thoughts. She's forgotten about the pistol under the counter.

Ardis comes in the next afternoon, and the next, and pretty soon he's in the habit of stopping by every day on his way home from the feed mill. Blanche sits behind the cash register. He leans against the counter next to the coffeemaker, his cold half-empty cup next to him. Blanche tends to feel a little low in the afternoons, when nobody comes by until school lets out at three and teenagers crowd in for the red hot dogs and the pool table, so she's not sorry to see Ardis then.

"When do you ever sleep?" asks Blanche.

"I steals me a nap now and then. I sleep in my car on my lunch break. I go to bed about eleven at night, set the alarm for one o'clock. Sleeping too much makes me lazy."

"Don't you just fall asleep when you get home?"

"If it's raining sometimes I'll lay down, but if it's nice out, I like to work in the yard."

"You got a big garden?"

"Used to. These days I make statues."

"What in the world of?"

"Car parts, mostly. I got a few junkers laying around. I saw 'em up with a welding torch and use the metal."

"Statues."

"Different animals. I'm in the middle of a mule right now."

"You sell 'em?"

"Naw. They too big for anybody to carry home. I just like making them."

Blanche pictures a yard crammed with rusting monsters. "Must be one hell of a sight," she says.

"I started making statues after I got out of the army," Ardis says. "I was sitting around on disability and getting kinda bored. Needed something to do with my hands." He chuckles. "Yeah, they done took over the garden. I got me a two-headed cow standing where the corn rows used to be."

"You still on disability?"

"Shhhhh," Ardis grins at her behind his upraised forefinger. "Don't tell no one. I work off the books. It ain't like the government check amounts to anything."

"Wish the government would send me a check instead of me giving money to them all the time."

"Well, now," Ardis looks down at his cup, "you might not want to pay the cost of getting the money."

"You get wounded?"

"Something like that." He won't tell her any more. When he leaves that afternoon, Blanche thinks she might see a slight limp, or it might just be her imagination. It doesn't look to her like there's anything wrong with the man at all.

On a day when it's pouring rain outside, the window of the station is so steamed up Blanche can barely make out Ardis' shadowy form scurrying across the gravel lot.

"I tell you," he says as the door clatters shut behind him, "I'm gonna get me a boat and paddle away from here." He hangs his wet jacket on a hook by the door. He's pulled a stool over from near the pool table and set it up next to the coffeemaker, keeping a safe distance between himself and Blanche. He pours himself a cup and settles in.

"No statue-making today I reckon," Blanche says.

"They can rust out there all by themselves, but you oughta come over and see them when the sun's shining."

"I couldn't leave the store."

"Sure you could. It ain't like anybody but me comes in here in the afternoon. Who's to know if you slipped away for an hour or two?"

The conversation makes Blanche uncomfortable. She changes the subject to something she's been wondering about. "You ever kill anybody in Viet Nam?"

"Not in Nam."

"You mean you killed somebody someplace else?"

"Had to."

"What do you mean, *had to?*"

"Boy was coming after my son. This was back when he was in high school. Boy said he stole his girlfriend and kept coming after him and threatening him and saying he was going to kill him. Deecy, that's my boy, was just about to get a football scholarship to college. I wasn't going to let some no-account punk take him away from me."

"You mean you shot him?"

"Yep. Caught him just as he was getting into his car in the high school parking lot. Surprised him."

"My goodness."

"I know it sounds bad, but the boy was going to kill my son. It wasn't just talk."

"Did you go to jail?"

"They let me go. I'm still on probation. Kid had been causing trouble for a long time. Wasn't nobody sorry to see him go."

Ardis gets down from his stool and pulls on his jacket. He walks back out into the rain. Blanche wonders what it would take to get her to kill somebody. Ardis' life holds a lot of secrets and surprises: war wounds he won't explain, murder, statues of animals. You'd never guess all that just looking at him.

Another afternoon. Blanche has come out from behind the counter to dust the shelves and the pool table. Ardis is perched on his stool. She thinks about losing weight, especially when she leans down to scoop a ball out from under the pool table and she can feel Ardis looking at her big butt. She straightens up and tosses the dusty ball onto the green felt.

"You married?" asks Ardis.

"My husband passed last year."

"I'm sorry to hear that. You got kids?"

"Two boys and a girl. Three handfuls."

Ardis laughs. "I hear you." He pulls a picture from his wallet. "This here's my baby girl." A gap-toothed child with braids all over her head. "She'll be in third grade this year."

Blanche takes the picture from him. "She's a cute little thing."

"Her name's Ardette."

"After you?"

He nods. "Her momma don't like it, but I don't stay with her momma no more so I don't mind."

"You get to see her much?"

"When she want something. Momma come first. Ardette just think I'm Mr. Cash. She the reason I have two jobs."

"She your only baby?"

"I got three grown boys...well, two grown and one just thinks he is. One got a baby of his own."

"Ol' grampaw."

"You got that right." Ardis smiles at her, his gold tooth gleaming. "The one that just thinks he's grown goes to Exeter."

"What's that?" asks Blanche.

"Private school up north. He's on scholarship too, and man I tell you he believes he's pretty hot stuff. Mr. Coat and Tie. He don't hardly like to come home no more."

Another scholarship. Blanche figures she's lucky if her kids can go to the local community college. Don't these people ever pay for anything they get? She shakes her head.

"I'll bring in pictures of my boys the next time I stop by," Ardis says proudly.

A few days later Ardis asks, "You ever date a black man?"

Blanche blushes to the roots of her bleached hair. "I don't believe in it," she says. "It ain't fair to the children."

"What if they didn't have children, would it be all right then?"

"No way."

"Why's that?"

There isn't any polite way to say because a white woman shouldn't lower herself. The smooth skin of Ardis' cheeks is very dark. "Black as my shoe" is what her grandmother used to say. He's got a brushy mustache and a square jaw. His eyes are warm and brown. His husky voice probably sends colored women over the edge. When she sits with him in the afternoon, part of Blanche enjoys Ardis' company, like he was any old fella stopped by to visit, like he was her neighbor Jack that she used to be a little sweet on. The other part of her takes in his nappy hair and shiny black skin and thinks the worst words about him. She says, "Colored women don't like it when you go outside the race, do they?"

He laughs. "My wife sure didn't."

Blanche used to hear that from the women at the mill. They get madder than she does when they see one of their men with a blonde on his arm. Shaquita's family didn't seem to think too highly of her seeing Bernard. "It's just curiosity," says Blanche. "It's not love."

"That right?" says Ardis.

"What kind of life could they have? Where would they hide? They'd have to go off to Chicago or somewheres."

"I know some staying back in the woods with their light-skinned babies all around the door. I know some see each other on the sly, drive clear to Raleigh to eat in a restaurant where nobody knows them."

"You sure know a lot about this."

"It's a whole nuther world out there, Blanche, a whole nuther world. Everybody pretends black and white don't get along, but they do just fine when it comes down to the main thing." He winks at her.

"That's still plain old dirty curiosity. Not love."

"There's folks been curious about each other a mighty long time then," he says.

Ardis doesn't show up for a week. Blanche listens for the sound of the Oldsmobile's tires on gravel every day. She hates waiting on somebody. She rearranges the shelves. The bread man will fuss at her since he likes his spot, but hell, there's only two aisles. Won't take a person that long to find everything there. On Thursday, she moves the coffeepot to a counter farther away from the cash register. She doesn't need people hanging around her while she's trying to work. She sticks Ardis' stool back in the corner behind the pool table. It's supposed to be for the pool players anyway. That's the thing about blacks: you never can count on them. They always have secrets, even while they grin at you for all they're worth. A lie is the same as the truth to them.

Blanche closes the store on Saturday evening. Sunday is her day off, which she usually looks forward to, but tonight it just feels like more of the same emptiness she's been sitting in all week. Maybe she'll take the kids somewhere, get away from the trailer for a little while. There's an air show over in Jacksonville might be worth going to.

The next Monday, Ardis shows up as though he hasn't been gone at all, but Blanche can smell the sweat and liquor on him from her chair behind the cash register. He makes his way to where the coffeepot used to be and stops, confused, before he looks around the room and sees it in its new location. He goes over to it, his movements slow and careful, as though something in him might break if he moves too fast. His hand shakes a little as he picks up the styrofoam cup. "See you done some redecorating," he says quietly.

"It was getting too crowded," says Blanche.

Since there's no stool to sit on anymore, he comes over to the cash register and leans against the wall next to the door. He hasn't shaved for a few days. Blanche will not ask him where he's been.

"How you been doing?" he asks.

"Fine. Went to an air show yesterday."

"Did you now. They have helicopters?"

"Yep. Quite a few."

"Did you see any of those Chinooks? They big, ain't they?"

Blanche nods.

"I had to go to the VA for my checkup," Ardis says.

"Must've been quite a checkup."

"That it was. They kept me there two days and ran a whole bunch of tests. You could hear the wind whistle through the puncture holes by the time they let me go."

Blanche has decided not to believe anything Ardis tells her. It's pretty damn clear what he's really been up to. "That right," she says.

"I'm off the hook for a couple more years now before I have to go back there," he says. It ain't like they doing a thing for me. I'm just one of their numbers. Keeps my government checks coming, though."

"You were up at the hospital Monday and Tuesday?"

"I got a little carried away when I came home. Sometimes old Jack Daniels won't leave me alone."

Finally, a piece of the truth.

"Good thing I stay out in the country all by myself or I'd get in real trouble." He takes another sip of coffee. "I hate that hospital."

"What is wrong with you?" blurts out Blanche, even though she has sworn not to encourage his lying with questions.

Ardis says nothing, just looks down at his cup. Then he starts talking about his damn statues, big hunks of metal Blanche doesn't ever intend to see.

16

It was still raining when I left Japonica-Smith. I felt a drop now and then on the back of my neck from a leak in the convertible's canvas roof I had never been able to track down. Out on the highway, a truck blew by, blinding me with its spray. My sense of adventure had palled. I was sick of driving, sick of looking for an angel who didn't want to be found. I had been on my own for twenty-four hours and nothing bad had happened to me yet. I suspected I was right about Phoebe's powers of protection being overblown.

I drove until I started passing strip malls on both sides of the road and the first traffic light I had seen in a while. I hadn't noticed a city limits sign yet. It appeared to be an army base, judging from the number of pawnshops, and barbers advertising MILITARY HAIRCUTS/4 DOLLARS. A gaudy storefront caught my eye: GAYLA TAVERN. It stood out from the grim pawnshops and dark bars like an artificial pink flower. I pulled into the parking lot.

Inside the Gayla a sparse group of happy hour drinkers was scattered among the tables. I settled myself on a bar stool. This would be Jo-Jo's kind of place, but instead of Shirley the bartender, a languid young man eased over and asked me what he could get me.

I ordered a beer and listened to the rain patter on the tin roof over us. I liked empty bars. They were like someone else's attic: full of memories you could only guess at. The odor of stale beer wafted up from the floor. Next to the mirror behind the bar were photographs of a drag contest. It was much too early in the day for Jo-Jo. He was probably just getting up now and shaving himself to prepare for his performance tonight.

Behind the bartender, a flicker of movement resolved itself into a winged form. His angel hovered like a shadow in the wrong place. I turned around on my stool and surveyed the other patrons with my new vision. They all had angels floating about their heads or settled in chairs next to their protectees. They didn't look like Phoebe. Some were blue or green or other nonhuman colors. Some were bald. One seemed like an old, old man. Another resembled a child. Apart from the hair that was a bit too red, Phoebe had looked pretty normal compared to these. The only things they had in common were wings and translucence. Was the difference in my imagination or in theirs?

It has been my experience that the people who are in a bar too early in the day either have a drinking problem or they're not from around there. I myself had just wandered in from the road, but the other denizens appeared as if they'd each been rooted to their particular spots for a long time.

There was a sad man in the far corner, drinking alone. Maybe he was a soldier—at least he had the right haircut, and was young. His angel leaned over him in a shadowy embrace. I supposed the sad man couldn't feel his angel's concern, or perhaps he could and was a little less sad for it. He stared at the air and shook his head before taking another long swallow of beer.

At a table close to his a group of three women were smoking and playing poker. Their angels floated above them in the cloud of smoke that emanated from the cigarettes. "Shitfire!" shouted one as another slapped down a full house. The first woman got up to buy the next round, her blue angel trailing closely behind.

The angels above the cardplayers' table were talking to each other and laughing at private, angel jokes. A whole other universe of camaraderie floated right over the human heads. No wonder Phoebe was so lonely and unhappy when she started to lose her angelic powers. She had no one to talk to except boring old me. One of the card-players' angels looked at me and pointed me out to the others. They all turned to stare. Self-consciously, I looked away. I didn't want to let them know I saw them.

I looked into the mirror through which no angels could be seen and I realized why the angels had noticed me. In the mirror you'd never guess that I was the only person in the room without an angel. I spun back around. When the cluster of angels realized that I could see them, they recoiled in fear. This was interesting. I remembered Phoebe's tales of psychopathic angel-less killers, but what could any human being do to an angel? I stood up and took a step toward them. They lurched backward like a flock of birds in a sudden gust. I want-ed to explain that I was accidentally alone, that I had been born with an angel by my side and had only recently lost track of her, but I was attracting enough attention as it was.

The cardplayers, unaware of the hysteria above, were idly gazing at me as though wondering what interesting and peculiar thing I would do next for their entertainment. The bartender was coming over to make sure I paid my tab before I took off for parts unknown. I supposed a little flying demo by me would wreak too much havoc on earth and in heaven. I sat back down, and the flock of angels set-tled together again over the cardplayers. They kept a wary eye on me, though. I ordered another beer so the bartender's trip wouldn't be wasted. The alcohol helped me ignore the music from above, which was starting to get on my nerves.

Outside, it was growing darker. The rain kept falling, hushing the sharp edges of the world. I put off thinking about dinner. I would leave when the bar got too noisy, unless I met someone I liked. The door from the parking lot opened and the bored bartender and I turned to see who it was. A hooded figure stood in the doorway a moment, its silhouette barely defined by the dimming grey light out-side. It was wearing a grey-green army poncho that bore a slight resemblance to a garbage bag. It pulled its hood back and a mass of curly black hair sprang up from its wearer's head. She looked familiar. As she stepped under the track light above the bar I recognized her as the woman with the camera at Japonica-Smith. I started to nod at her, then stopped in fright. She had no angel. Behind me I could hear the frantic fluttering of angel wings over the poker table. They must really be panicked now that there were two of us. I backed off to a stool on the far corner of the bar.

The woman looked straight at me as though she knew me and was waiting for me to speak. She didn't smile. Had she followed me all the way here? What did she want? I tried to be cool. I kept on sipping my beer, ignoring her, though that was a little difficult since she sat at the other end of the bar directly in my line of vision. Could she see that I didn't have an angel either? Her eyes were as black as her hair. Her stare was getting to me. I plopped down a few bills to pay for my beers, grabbed my jacket, and got out of there.

I drove too fast down the wet road. In the cloud of spray behind the car I couldn't make out whether or not anyone was following me. If the woman was indeed a psychopath, no one, not even Phoebe, knew where I was. Drops from the leaky roof spattered my neck, making me start each time they fell. Where could I hide? Maybe I should go back home, although I had become so entangled in my sinistration I had no idea what direction home was in, or even what the name was of the town I had just fled. My pursuer arrived at the bar so long after I got there, it seemed as though she hadn't followed me, but simply knew where I was going. I wish she would tell me. I drove on into the darkness.

CARLA MOVES FROM BOX TO box to box now, working on three stories at once. There are lots of boxes of the angel. Next to the box where the motorcycle rider is tearing down the grey ribbon of road, Carla starts putting things into another box. Phoebe is in a K-Mart, in the hair section. She's picking up hair fasteners from the shelves and slipping them into the pockets of her borrowed leather jacket. A mirror and a bottle of perfume tumble in after the hair fasteners. Carla filched the tiny bottle from a box of Barbie accessories at Toys'R'Us. It has real, noxious perfume in it.

In the next box, the angel has moved on to makeup. Lipstick and eyeshadow are very easy to steal. She seems unaware that there might be cameras overhead, or mirrors through which other eyes could observe her. Another box. Now she's in the men's aisle, bottles of Brut and Grecian Formula clinking into her pockets. She finishes up with a return to the women's section and a can of hairspray and a comb. With the leather jacket ballooned out and rattling, she wanders nonchalantly toward the entrance to the store. Three men in uniform wait for her there.

The grand tussle fills up an entire box: Phoebe kicking and biting and pulling hair, the men in their rented security uniforms trying to keep a grip on her. Her mouth is drawn in a shout. The cashiers watch in fascination. The glass door at the front of the store breaks and Phoebe dashes out through the opening to her bike. She flies off down the road, zipping between trucks, bottles and plastic boxes cascading from her pockets and shattering on the asphalt.

My FEAR WAS MAKING ME crazy. I tried to convince myself that the woman with the curly hair was only human, that I didn't see her behind me in the spray lit red by my taillights. I took every turn I saw—right or left, it didn't matter. The point was to keep moving fast enough to stay ahead of her. If I didn't know where my destination was, she wouldn't be able to predict it and catch up with me there. The raindrops blew silver in front of the car.

I glanced down at my fuel gauge and looked up in a panic for a gas station. The needle hovered just above E. How much did I have left after it passed Empty? I couldn't remember whether I had one of those little warning lights that tell you you've only got a gallon left. In my former life, I had been a much more careful person and had never had less than half a tank. Frogs were hopping all over the wet pavement in the rain. I'd see their little bodies leap up in the headlights just before I killed them. I started to cry—for the dead frogs, for my lost self, for Phoebe, who was lost, too. And somewhere in the night ahead of me or behind me in the windy dark was a woman who had no angel and who knew who I was.

The greenish glow of a gas station sign beckoned before I slowed down and saw the place was closed. Wherever I was, there was no one out here. I must be running on fumes by now. Another cluster of buildings flickered ahead through the windshield wipers. I cried again with relief when I saw cars parked outside a brightly lit convenience store. I pulled next to the pump and tried to make myself presentable by wiping my wet face on my shirtsleeve. I peered at myself in the rearview mirror: a frightened, weepy woman looked pleadingly back. I pumped gas and dashed through the rain into the store to pay.

There were angels inside, standing shadows next to all the customers there. They pulled away from me just as the flock in the bar had. There was one floating a little above and behind a farmer pondering the contents of the beer cooler. It fluttered frantically until I whispered to it, "Please. Help me. I've lost my angel." The angel looked at me sympathetically and shrugged. I can't, it mouthed. It glanced sideways at its charge, who had decided on a twelve-pack of Old Milwaukee. I turned and scanned the store for help. The other angels were now more curious than frightened. They must've heard my whispered explanation. They watched me the way children observe a crippled child at a playground. They were interested, they perhaps even pitied me, but they all had their assigned people from whose sides they could not stray. I went up to each angel, no longer caring how bizarre I must seem to the attached human. Each one shook its head and smiled a regretful smile. They probably thought it was pretty careless of me to lose my angel. If I was going to be protected, I would have to find an angel who had no person. Phoebe was the only one on earth who fit that description.

When I pushed open the glass doors to go back out to my car, the wind was colder and it was raining harder. I was soaked to the bone. Far above the rain and the wind, I could just barely hear the silver note. It was all I had now.

In her box, the angel is looking into a tiny silver mirror. Jars and bottles are scattered all around her. Her plastic hand is raised in front of her face to apply purple eye shadow. Another box, another scene: the angel, in love with her image, is admiring the results of her cosmetic endeavors. Carla imagines her whispering, "Pretty, pretty." On this particular evening, Carla is working only on the boxes of the self-absorbed angel. She leaves the one with the mirror to her own fascination and starts a new box, this one with a restaurant sign she painted last night: WILLARD'S ALL-U-CAN-EAT BARBECUE PIT. WE LOVE CHILDREN! She arranges chairs and tables inside and places another plastic Phoebe at a table scattered with half-empty plates and chicken bones. She is eating, her face close to her plate. She shovels shredded pork into her mouth with both fork and hand. Her cheeks are puffed out and shiny with grease. Phoebe interrupts her gluttony to signal the waitress for another platter of fried chicken. Her wings are completely gone.

In the next scene, a potbellied Phoebe waddles out of Willard's door and across the gravel parking lot toward her motorcycle. Above her three angels are floating. She stares up at them enviously, too heavy to fly.

DRIVING ALL NIGHT DOES STRANGE things to you. Somewhere in the early morning, I didn't notice when, the rain had stopped. The windshield wipers squealed back and forth for a long time before I realized where the noise was coming from, or even that there was a noise. I was outside of myself, which I suppose is a dangerous way to drive, although I didn't collide with anything so far as I was aware. Time had shattered into discontiguous pieces. I would be in the present, then I would lose track of it on some mental rambling until I returned with a start to what was supposedly now, not knowing where I'd been for the last fifteen minutes. All I knew was that I had to keep moving.

AM radio in the dark of the morning is mostly call-in shows from faraway places like Buffalo or Indiana. I listened to the voices of people as lonely and frightened as I was, with opinions no one wanted to hear. As my exhaustion grew, I stopped feeling anything.

In the east, and I did seem to be driving east at that moment, the sky turned pink and yellow to light the undersides of hanging clouds. I rolled down my window to breathe the innocent morning air. Birds were calling to each other in arcs from tree to tree. Morning was a time when salvation seemed possible, even if you had been running from impending doom all night. I picked up coffee at a truck stop. I wasn't hungry. I inhaled deeply; the air itself was sweet enough to sustain me. Surely no harm could befall me in this light.

My headlong flight turned into aimless wandering. I wasn't looking for anything since somewhere in the night I had given up on Phoebe, and I wasn't fleeing anything since I had just grown plain tired of being scared and decided not to be anymore.

The sun was a quarter of its way up the sky and behind me when I came into a town of big brick warehouses. The air smelled of tobacco as the machinery inside the plants rolled out their cigarettes. I lit one and peered into the crumpled pack. I only had one cigarette left; I had forgotten to pick up more when I got my coffee. I may have been able to live on air, but only if it had enough smoke in it. Despite the heavenly scent all around me, I didn't see any place where I could actually purchase cigarettes until a mile or so later, where I came across a little strip mall with a drugstore. On my way out of the store, I noticed a photographer's studio. A portrait of a well-to-do black couple was presented in the window that reminded me of Jo-Jo's final portrait. While it was true I had given up on Phoebe, I still wanted to make Jo-Jo's acquaintance. Maybe this was Max's studio and Max could tell me where Jo-Jo was.

The portrait was an awful lot like the last one Phoebe had written for Jo-Jo: stiff formal man in back, smiling woman wearing a frilly dress in front. She lacked a gold tooth, but I supposed I could allow real life a little artistic license. The two didn't actually resemble each other that much. Jo-Jo was better at impersonation than I had given him credit for. I pushed open a clouded glass door not unlike the one that belonged to Max. It was just after ten o'clock.

There were photographs hung on both walls of the hallway that were not at all like the portrait of Jo-Jo.

There was a little girl, her dark eyes filled with pain beyond my understanding, pinned beneath the fallen timbers of her house. In another picture, a band of soldiers stood against the green backdrop of a jungle, their shiny grey metal guns cradled casually in their arms or resting on their slim hips. Only a couple of them were old enough to grow a mustache. They were sinewy from starvation and fighting. In front of them were arranged a collection of torn corpses. The tropical sunlight caressed the soldiers and the dead. Next to the soldiers' portrait, a group of women mourned the death of their sons in Bosnia. They were positioned like standing statues, their faces carved in stone.

I looked at those pictures and saw my own soul's anguish mirrored. Most disturbing about them was the fact that they were so beautiful. I couldn't stop myself from going into their depths even as I tried to tear my eyes away from this marriage of heaven and hell.

There were also photographs whose hellishness was not as apparent. In one was the flared cone of a nuclear power plant, photographed across a misty lake in early morning. It appeared to rise out of the water like a swan or a spray of white foam. In front of the cone, a ragged line of terns flew over the water's surface. From the white of the power plant billowed a cloud of steam in a brighter white, rising hundreds of feet into the air before it dissipated into the pale blue of the sky. The morning sun cast a pinkish tone on one edge of the vertical cloud.

Another photograph was taken at night. The bottom half of the picture was a swirl of car lights, brakelights and headlights flowing in opposite currents. In the upper half, where the currents converged, the flecked towers of a far-off city interrupted a cobalt blue sky. The sun had recently set; there was still a tinge of light in the dome overhead.

The pictures without people were like evidence of crimes committed long ago. You had to look for the flaw contained within the lovely facade. The sole black-and-white photograph was of a desert littered with rusting metal drums faintly embossed with the symbol for radioactivity. The sharp outlines of the drums' shadows reached across the white sand. The scene had all the spareness and beauty of a Japanese rock garden.

I heard the door at the far end of the hall open and I turned to say hello to Max. Standing in the doorway was the woman I had been running from all night. I moved down the narrow corridor away from her, walking backward as fast as I could without actually running. She merely watched as I exited, much too slowly, down the long corridor toward the glass door and safety.

"They're 'Beautiful Terrors,'" she said.

I shook my head without comprehending the words, "No, no," I said. "Go away. I don't know you."

"The photographs you were looking at. I've named them 'Beautiful Terrors.'"

"That's nice," I said. I clasped the reassuring sphere of the doorknob and started to turn it.

"Please," she said. "I have more you can see."

"What?"

"More pictures. I think you'd like them."

From my safer distance, she looked smaller and a bit forlorn. The pounding of my blood in my ears slowed. Although I hadn't yet tried out my new angelic powers as a means of escape, I could probably fly away if she got too close.

"Terrors?" I said.

"I was driving across the lake in the early morning and I saw the power plant and before I could reflect too much on what it was and what it meant I just thought it was pretty and then I thought it would be interesting to take beautiful pictures of bad things because anything can be beautiful, really, if you just look at it in the right way." She said this fast and quietly.

The woman was clearly delusional. "Like this picture here," she said. She pointed to the river of light made by the cars. "This bypass was built over farmland that had been owned by the same families for a hundred years. The runoff has killed all the life in the stream that flows under it. And the road itself is dangerous. There'd been three fatal wrecks in the month before I took this picture. I saw them carry the body bags away from the last one. Did you know body bags are yellow?"

Now there was an interesting tidbit. I wondered why she hadn't taken pretty photos of crumpled cars and mangled corpses. "Very nice," I said.

"I need to add a caption." She frowned and moved a bit down the hallway to study her work. My grip on the doorknob tightened. I hadn't yet determined if she was nutty and dangerous or merely nutty. "You wouldn't know about the scary part unless you recognized the road or I explained it to you."

"Have you been following me?" I asked.

"Sometimes," she said. "But sometimes you've found me. Like this morning."

"Did you follow me from the bar?"

"Oh, no. It was much too bad a night to be driving around and, besides, I had no idea where you'd gone. I thought I would probably never see you again."

"Who are you?" I asked.

"My name's Morgan."

I waved away the answer. "I don't care what your name is. Who *are* you?"

"What do you mean?"

"*Why* are you following me?"

"When I saw you flying over the field, I had to know who you were. You're the only other person I've ever seen up there."

"That was you?" It seemed much longer ago than yesterday morning that I saw the dark figure suspended in the distance.

Morgan stepped to another picture and examined it. "It was hard to get the lighting just right on this one." She gestured toward the corpses clad in ruby blood. I could see Morgan adjusting her lamps around the dead, and I shuddered.

"Why don't you have an angel?" I asked.

"Do you believe in angels? I used to when I was a little kid but I don't anymore."

"You didn't see them when you were flying over the field?"

She smiled as though laughing at herself. "Sometimes I think I hear the fluttering of wings, but it's just birds. I can hear the whistling sound the wind makes when I'm up there."

My curiosity had overcome my own terror and I let go of the doorknob. There was no flicker of an angel anywhere in the air around Morgan, but she just didn't seem as scary as Phoebe had made people like her out to be.

"I only learned to fly a few weeks ago," I said. If Morgan didn't think angels existed, my explanation of how I learned probably wouldn't be very convincing.

"That's interesting." She looked at me quizzically. "I didn't know it could be learned. I've always known how to fly, ever since I could stand upright."

"That must've given your mother fits. Walking babies are hard enough to handle."

"Oh, I wasn't raised by my mother. But even when I was a baby I had sense enough to know grownups wouldn't like it. I would wait until after all the other girls were asleep before I stood up in my bed and floated to the ceiling. I didn't want them to tell on me. I grew up in an orphanage. They call them Homes, but an orphanage was what it was."

"Sounds quite Dickensian," I said.

"Yes," she said, without elaboration. "Why don't you come into the studio? You look a little tired."

Too tired, evidently, to be very worried about being alone in a back room with a psychotic. I followed her down the hall. "You must travel a lot to take all those pictures," I said.

"Being able to fly helps."

Ah. Maybe up and down weren't the only directions I could go. I remembered a comment Phoebe made during my flying lesson. "How about astral projection?"

"Of course," Morgan said as she closed the door behind us. "If I want to go any distance, it would take too long to simply fly."

In a corner of the studio were a silver aluminum kitchenette and a cot. An upended orange crate at the foot of the bed held neatly folded clothes. On a table at the head of the bed were a reading lamp and a stack of photography magazines. Morgan poured the dregs of a coffeepot into two mugs. Her back was toward me. She was wearing a blue plaid flannel shirt that went nicely with her black hair. She was a bit taller than I was, a bit more angular.

The rest of the large room was filled with photographic equipment: cameras on tripods, big lights, white screens. Wires crisscrossed the floor. Morgan motioned me toward the cot. "Have a seat. Watch your step."

"Nice apartment."

She smiled. "Since I spend most of my time here, it would be silly to pay extra to rent a place." I was so tired I leaned back across the bed and rested my head on the drywall behind me. I felt safer than I had felt since Phoebe's disappearance, despite the gruesome pictures and Morgan's lack of a spiritual companion. I felt safe because there was nowhere else to run. Morgan handed me a mug and I sat up to sip the bitter coffee. She sat down on the folding chair next to the bed. I waited for her story to unfold.

"Did you have parents?" she asked.

"Yes," I said. "Perfectly nice ones."

She nodded. "That's why you couldn't fly when you were little."

"How's that?"

"I always figured I could fly because I didn't have any parents.

Some of the other children in the orphanage could fly, too. I saw them after they thought I'd fallen asleep."

I pictured toddlers in nightgowns floating up from their beds in a moonlit nursery, rising and falling and chortling quietly to themselves. "I could see my guardian angel when I was little," I said. Now it was Morgan's turn to look disbelieving.

"You actually think they're real, don't you?"

"Why not? You believe babies levitate."

"Well, we both know we can fly. We saw each other out there."

I didn't argue the existence of Phoebe. It's not like I could cause her to suddenly appear to prove my point. "What happened to your parents?" I asked, a little rudely, because I was annoyed with Morgan's obstinacy and because I wanted to change the subject.

"I don't know. They could still be alive."

"But you were in an orphanage," I pointed out.

"Lost parents might as well be dead," she said. "It was a long time before anyone would tell me where I'd come from. The closest hint I got was when one of the counselors said I'd been found under a cabbage leaf. Of course, she said the same thing to all of us, but in my case it was true." She seemed amused by some private joke.

"A cabbage leaf?" I said.

"Finally I turned eighteen and was just about to graduate from high school and leave the place when the director arranged to see me in her office. This was a rite of passage for getting out of the orphanage. Nobody knew what went on in the director's office, but everybody got called in there when it was time to go."

She blew on her coffee, although it must've been cool enough by this point. I put my mug on the table next to the bed and leaned back, waiting to hear more.

"I thought that it would just be another pep talk about going into the real world, away from the family of the Home, and how she would never forget any of us and I must always keep in touch and let her know how I was doing because all of her girls were just like daughters to her. The director always talked like that.

"My appointment was in the afternoon, after school. There was this miserable hard wooden bench that you sat on outside her office while you waited. The director made sure you were there awhile before she called you in.

"So I waited. Part of me thought I should just fly away from there, but I was also a little curious about what the director would actually say. Even though I thought I knew, everyone was so damned secretive about it that my interest was piqued."

"Why didn't you fly away from the orphanage before then?"

Morgan nodded as though she'd already asked herself that question. "I certainly could have. Some of the other girls did. The counselors told us they ran away, but I knew better. The director was right in spite of herself: we really were a family. Shitty as the place was, the Home was the only one I had."

"What did the director say to you?"

"When she called me in fifteen minutes after I was scheduled, she had a big green folder with my name on it on her desk. She said, 'Good afternoon, Morgan,' in this prissy, imperious way she had. Then she went on and on about how these were my records and now it was time for me to know the circumstances of my birth. I'd listened to that voice my whole life and I'd gotten into the habit of ignoring everything it said, so when I heard the word *records* it took a while before I realized she wasn't talking about my school records. She was talking about where I came from."

"Why was it such a big secret?"

Morgan shrugged. "It was the way the place was. None of us knew who her real family was, or why she was there, because we were one big happy family. We were supposed to pretend the director was our grandmother and the counselors were our mommies. We all knew better, of course. Kids aren't stupid.

"Since they would never tell us anything, there were always rumors flying around about how we'd been kidnapped, and pretty soon our real parents would find out where we were and rescue us. I even believed them for a while."

"So what did the director say?"

"After her little speech, she pushed the folder toward me and peered at me over these reading glasses she wore on a chain draped around her neck. 'Feel free to examine the contents, dear,' she said. So

I did, under that horrible kindly gaze. I went right to the beginning of the folder—the one thing I had figured out was that I'd been in the orphanage since I was a baby. There were a lot of reports with scrawled handwriting from Social Services. I found my birth certificate. My name used to be Baby Doe."

"I like Morgan better."

"So do I. There was one piece of paper filed even before the birth certificate. The paper described where I came from."

Okay, so I was sitting up now. "And?"

"My parents threw me away."

"What?"

"I was found in a garbage can. My mother must've tossed me in there the minute she gave birth to me."

I gasped.

"It's amazing they even found me, isn't it?"

Morgan had no idea how amazing it was. "Someone heard you crying," I said.

"Must have," she said.

"Lucky for you." I wished Phoebe had been there to hear this story. The lost baby had haunted her so. Morgan was right. I had been looking for her.

"I don't know if it was lucky or not," Morgan said. "I've always felt too open to the world. It's like I see everything, including things other people don't. That's what the camera is for, to come between me and what I see."

"Maybe you're missing the mother you never knew," I said.

"Maybe," she said, but she didn't sound too sure. "It's almost as though I see through everything. Like with the nuclear power plant, my friends think it's ugly and awful because of what it is, and I guess a nuclear advocate would think it was just the greatest thing, but even he probably wouldn't see the beauty of it the way I do, only the functionality. I see the way metal shimmers in the rain after a car accident, and the contrast of the dark red blood flowing over the dark grey pavement."

Either my tiredness or Morgan's philosophy was making me dizzy. Or she'd slipped a Mickey into my coffee after all. She was sitting on the chair across from me, her elbows on her knees, her face cupped in her hands. I guessed it would have been rude for me to fall asleep on a virtual stranger's bed.

"Why don't you try to sleep?" she asked.

"No, no, I'd better be going."

"Where will you go?

Where indeed. I'd found my doppelgänger and lost my angel. There wasn't much else to look for. "What day is it?" I asked. I seemed to remember a job or something I had to get back to.

"Sunday," she said.

"Only Sunday?" I yawned.

"Stay here," she said. "I'll be quiet. You really shouldn't be driving." She slipped the mug from my hand and patted the pillow. "Lie down."

18

Pretty soon the stool is over by the coffeepot in Blanche's store, and the coffeepot is back near the cash register. Ardis keeps coming in, just like always except for the week he missed. Blanche would like to point out to him that he might have mentioned he'd be going somewhere, but that sounds too much like the things she used to say to Ervin after he'd come back from drinking with his buddies. Nag, nag, nag. She can hear herself, and so she doesn't say anything. Sure would be nice if she could just up and leave for a week without telling anybody, but she has responsibilities. She does let herself ask one question: "Who covered your paper route?"

"Anthony, my oldest. He stay right next to me."

They all live together, just like in Georgetown.

"Must be hard raising them kids alone," Ardis says.

"I get by. In a few years they'll be grown and gone, then I can relax."

"You'll miss 'em though."

"I'm looking forward to the day the last bird is out of the nest. Once they graduate high school, they're on their own."

"And you'll be on your own and lonesome."

"I'm on my own now," says Blanche. "Ain't like nobody's helping me out."

"You ever think about getting married again?"

"I don't know. Men make such a mess. I'm stretched enough picking up after the kids."

"Men are only good for one thing, huh? That's what my wife used to tell me."

Blanche pretends she doesn't understand. "Yeah, they can lift big boxes."

Ardis laughs and winks at her. "Two things, then," he says. She tries not to smile back.

"I bet you have a girlfriend," Blanche says.

"Naw. I gets into too much trouble with women. Too much trouble...." Something comes to mind and he shakes his head with the memory. "I can't believe *you* don't have a boyfriend. You must be swattin' them off like flies."

"I wish," says Blanche. No one looks at you after you pass thirty-five, unless they want you to refill their coffee. Even the old men want a teenager.

"There're a whole bunch of fools out there if they ain't coming to sniff around your door. You step out every Saturday night?"

"With my girlfriends. We go down to the Holiday Inn and drink a little wine."

"Talk about men, don't you?" Ardis laughed.

"How they ain't no good and we should stay the hell away from them."

"You wouldn't be talking about 'em if you weren't interested in 'em, now would you?"

"Nothing else to talk about in this place. Not like anything ever happens."

"Love is all there is to talk about anywhere," says Ardis. He touches Blanche's shoulder as he passes by her on his way out the door. "I'll be seeing you tomorrow."

In the morning, Blanche takes more time than usual in the bathroom. She stares into the mirror, noticing new jowls along her chin and new lines around her mouth. She tries to do something about them with makeup, but it makes her look a damn fright, like she's been to the undertaker's. She needs to do her hair this weekend. Her roots are starting to show. She gets dressed; her slacks are too tight around the waist. Shannon complains her smoking makes the car stink, but she lights a cigarette while she's driving to work anyway. She's late, and Ardis is there waiting for her. He holds the screen door open for her while she fiddles with the lock.

"You looking fine this morning," he says.

"That's a lie."

"Whoo!" He follows her into the dark store. "Don't pay to give some people compliments. How about I make the coffee and bring you some? That might improve your state of mind." He glances at his watch. "I'm running late." He brings her a cup on his way out the door. Ardis is wearing a cologne that just brushes the air with sweetness. Blanche can still smell it long after the Oldsmobile has rumbled away.

There's a reason for the way the traffic flows by the store that Blanche can't figure out. Tuesday afternoons are always slow. Thursdays it gets right crowded. What makes people go somewhere all at once? Today is a Tuesday. She's pretty bored by the time Ardis comes by. She stifles a yawn just as he's walking in.

"Wake up, you got company," he says.

"Might as well not even be open on Tuesday afternoons," says Blanche.

"Well now, it's better than the mill, ain't it?"

"I guess. At least I had somebody to talk to at the mill."

"Here I am. You can talk to me." He perches on his stool. "You want to go see my statues?" he asks.

"You know I can't leave the store."

"Sure you can. Nobody'll be by until the high school lets out. You got time. I stay just down the road."

"No, no." But Blanche is wavering. It's not like she would lose any business.

"Come on. It's a fine day."

She stands up and pulls her cardigan off the back of her chair.

"There you go. Get out into the sunshine. You don't need that sweater."

She brings it with her anyway. She stands outside the passenger door. "That door don't open from the outside," he says. He slips in from the driver's side and leans over the seat to pop her door open. One of those green tree things that smells worse than the old car odor it's trying to cover up hangs from the rearview mirror. The clear plastic seats of the Olds are striped with duct tape. A newish radio is stuck in where the old one used to be. There are gaps around the edge where it doesn't fit. When Ardis turns the engine on, a heavy bass thump from the speakers blasts through the car. He quickly turns the volume down. "Sorry about that," he says. "I crank it up when I'm driving by myself." Blanche gropes around for a seat belt and doesn't find one. Ardis is so short he has the seat pushed all the way up and she feels like her chin is resting on the dashboard. Blanche is suddenly aware of what anyone would think if they saw them, a black man and a white woman in the front seat of the same car. It's not what people would think, but that's the way it would look.

A mile or so down the road Ardis pulls into a rutted dirt lane that's like a tractor road going back to the next field, but as the big car edges and wobbles over the ruts, scattered houses start to appear in the pine woods on either side: tarpaper shacks and cinderblock squares, an old sharecropper's cabin with the porch sagging, a trailer, a two-story brick house that looks like somebody built it all by himself.

At the end of the road, a gang of three dogs rushes from behind the house to bark at the windows of the car. "Git outta here." Ardis opens the door and shoves them aside. "They won't bite," he says to Blanche.

She pushes on the door handle, and it opens with a grinding squeal. The dogs rush around to see what the awful noise is and bark more furiously when they see her white face. She pulls the door shut against them.

"I'll put 'em up," says Ardis. The dogs follow him to a pen around the side of the house and he shoos them in. The beagle that lives at Blanche's house goes crazy when he sees a colored person. Animals know the difference between their own kind and what's not their own kind.

"You can come out now." Ardis grins at her through the window. She pushes the door open and pulls herself up out of the seat. The house appears to be three houses stuck together, all different colors. There's a turquoise trailer in the middle, with a wooden wing tacked onto either end. One wing is painted white, and the other might have been painted once upon a time, but now it's grey wood with a few white streaks. "My wife called this place On and On, 'cause it just goes on and on," he says. "I kept adding to it so it would be big enough to hold the kids."

The grass around Ardis' house blows in the breeze. A red mower sits rusting in the long grass by the front porch. Paths lead here and there through the lawn, back to the dog pen, where the dogs are frantic to get out, to the side door of the house, and into an overgrown field. "Come on, I'll show you what I been talking about," Ardis says as he walks toward the field. Blanche follows him, being careful of where she steps; the path is a muddy trough from the recent rains. She sees the shapes of things through the tall grass, half-seen shadows that might be anything—animals, people, or forgotten farm machinery. "I need to fix that mower," Ardis says.

They turn off onto a smaller path, just a trace of footsteps that leads to the spined thing, which turns out to be a dinosaur of rough brown metal. It's mostly a dinosaur, except it has the head of a cat. Red flecks of paint cling to the rust of the metal. "This old stuff was sitting around," he says. "I figured I might as well do something with it."

The wet mud of the path squishes beneath Blanche's white shoes. "This field ever flood?" she asks.

"Every spring and every fall," Ardis answers. "The river's right over there." He points in a direction from which she can hear the whisper of water flowing.

"Doesn't it come into your house?" she asks.

"Sometimes. When it does, I go on up the road and stay with one of my sons. And clean up afterwards."

She follows him down another path. He points out an angular

bull with a purple painted head and a wriggling snake twenty feet tall. "I laid it out on the ground first, then I pulled it up with a winch." Smaller metal creatures peek out here and there. She almost trips over an armadillo whose nose protrudes into the path. They walk farther and farther from the house and the car and closer to the sound of the river. The statues loom everywhere in the grass.

"What the hell happened here?" asks Blanche. They've reached a trampled-down circle. A statue of a giant man lies toppled over, its twisted metal arms pushing into the soft earth. All around the man is a band of broken glass, some of it whole enough to reveal the shoulders and labels of whiskey bottles.

"I got a little carried away the week I had off," says Ardis.

"I should say."

"Some days drinking is the only cure for what ails you." He pokes at the shards with his foot. "They won't tell me what's wrong with me, but they keep paying me, so I reckon they know. Some bug or chemical they sprayed me with in Nam that won't ever leave me alone. That's how come my wife is gone," he says quietly. "The pain wouldn't let her be neither. She could move out the house and leave it behind. I can't."

Blanche puts her hand on his dark arm for the first time. There's a sheen to his skin, and hardly any hair. "What's hurting you?" she asks.

"They tell me it's just memories, but there's something else going on. Memories don't make your skin feel like it wants to crawl away from the rest of you. They don't make your brain feel like it's on fire. I got memories, too, but I can handle them." His voice breaks.

"You could of told me before," she says.

"Bet you thought my thing got shot off."

Blanche doesn't want to admit that's what she thought.

"Everybody thinks that when you don't tell 'em what's wrong with you. Nope, everything's still attached."

They stand together at the edge of Ardis' sad altar, Blanche stroking his arm. "I best be going back," she says.

"You ain't seen all the statues yet."

"The high school's about to let out. I got to go open the store."

When she turns around, she can hear Ardis' footsteps behind her. She thinks she can feel his breath on the back of her neck, as soft as the cologne he wears. "Hold on just a minute," Ardis says. He grabs Blanche's hand. What she notices most is the roughness of the skin. It's been since long before Ervin died that she's held hands with anybody. She and Ervin didn't touch much, except quickly in the night sometimes. She was holding Ervin's hand when he died; his skin was just as rough as Ardis'. She turns to look at him, but she glances down instead because she's suddenly feeling shy. Now that she's facing him, he takes her other hand. "Let's not go so soon," he says. "Let's you and me stay here a little while."

"I've got to get back," Blanche says, without conviction.

"Come on now," says Ardis. He kisses her cheek lightly, like a butterfly. It's been so long. Without thinking, Blanche rubs her thumb along the back of his hand, tracing the two veins that intertwine there. Close to him like this, she smells his metallic sweat combined with soap beneath the scent of his cologne. He's a clean man. His chin is smooth-shaven. He kisses her again, this time on the mouth, just as gently as he brushed her cheek. "Stay here," he says once more.

Reluctantly, Blanche pulls away. "I depend on that store," she says. "I'm short of cash this week." Together they follow the path out of the field. Ardis holds her hand as they walk together, the grasses whispering around them. She waits outside his car until he pops the door open for her from the inside. On the ride back down the road he says, "You busy tonight?"

"I'm taking Shannon to choir practice."

"Maybe some other night then."

She nods without thinking about it too much. "I hate what they did to you," she says.

There are customers waiting when they pull into the parking lot in front of the store, white teenagers who smirk when they see Blanche get out of a colored man's car. One of them makes a kissing sound behind her back as she unlocks the door. She hears the Oldsmobile pull away. She doesn't have a chance to watch Ardis leave, the boys are piling in so fast to get to the pool table.

"That nigger your new boyfriend, Blanche?" one of them says as he racks the balls. The rest cluster around him, watching her.

"Shut up," she says. "He was just giving me a ride."

"Why didn't you come to me if you were that desperate? I'da taken care of you." They laugh in loud whoops. "Yeah, I'da given you a ride." He's a boy that can barely grow a mustache.

"Don't you wish," says Blanche. "You best run home to Momma before you miss your afternoon nap." She grabs a broom and advances toward the pool players. "I'm closing up. Get out of here, all of you." They stand still for a minute, not believing her, until Blanche uses the broom to smack a pool cue out of one of their hands. "Get out."

"Where's my hot dog?"

"You shoulda thought about your hot dog before you messed with me. Out."

She shoves the last one through the door and locks it shut behind him. She pulls the blinds over the window, but not before she sees them cluster in the parking lot, looking back at her and punching each other in the shoulder and laughing. Damn them all. Damn Ardis. She waits until their jacked-up cars have left before she leaves the store herself.

Blanche stops by the Winn-Dixie on the way home to pick up pork chops for dinner. She passes a black boy and a white girl holding hands on their way out of the store. It ain't right. Blanche feels herself coming back into herself from wherever she's been all afternoon; she slips into her old rage. She snaps her head around to glare at the couple. The black boy catches her eye and winks. She stares back at him, letting him know what she thinks. The very idea sickens her.

She's ready for Ardis the next morning, only he's in a hurry and just stops by to get coffee without saying much. His fingers brush hers as he hands her the money. She won't look up. "Thank you. You have a good day," she says, as I-don't-care-who-you-are as she can.

"You, too, Blanche. You, too. I'll be seeing you this afternoon." Ardis has what you might call a bedroom voice.

She's ready for him again when he comes in in the afternoon. "Hey there," he says. He stands next to the cash register, waiting.

"Can I help you with something?" Blanche asks coldly.

"You ain't forgotten yesterday afternoon already, have you?"

"I didn't forget nothing. We didn't do nothing, and we ain't gonna do nothing."

Ardis settles back on his stool. "We didn't harm nobody, Blanche."

"You stay away from me. You blacks are always coming after white women. Why can't you stick with your own kind?"

"Well, now, I wasn't the only one coming after anybody yesterday."

"That's a damn lie. I was looking at your statues and you started hittin' on me. I didn't go out to your place for that."

"You mean you didn't like my sugar? That ain't the way you acted."

"You don't need to come here anymore. There's a store just down the road where you can get your coffee."

Ardis stands up from his stool. "You mean it?"

"I surely do. You been hanging around too much."

Ardis walks slowly to the door. "All right, then," he says softly. The screen door slaps shut behind him for the last time.

Blanche busies herself around the store straightening, dusting, taking inventory. She slips a copy of the *Weekly World News* from the rack and settles down with another cup of coffee and a cigarette. She doesn't believe a word of it. She's careful not to muss the pages so she can stick the *News* back in the rack when she's done. The road out front is still; the afternoon sun dapples it in sunlight and shadow. In the peace of the empty store, Blanche listens to her life slip by.

IT TAKES SOME EFFORT FOR Phoebe to wriggle into the second-story window of Alice's apartment. It's almost light enough by now to see her as she balances on the narrow ledge below the window and works a screwdriver up between the sashes to spring the lock. Alice is too damned careful about locking all the windows. It's the second floor for God's sake, who would try to break in here? While she's teetering on the ledge and sweating, Phoebe considers that she should have broken through the door instead, except she was afraid the noise in the hallway would wake everybody. She's not as practiced at this as she'd like to be.

Getting up here was no joke. She stood in the dark parking lot a long time trying to figure it out. She'd been riding down the empty road, going nowhere in particular, when she had the idea of dropping into Alice's bedroom while she was asleep and surprising her. She forgot she couldn't fly anymore. She just thought she'd float up and slip through the window. As it was, she had to wheel her bike right up to the front entrance, stand on the seat, and pull herself onto the little roof over the steps. She seems to have put on some weight. She barely managed to drag herself on top of the asphalt shingles.

The lock finally gives. Phoebe clenches the screwdriver between her teeth, pushes the sash up, and tumbles into Alice's bedroom. Alice's empty bed is neatly made. The sun isn't even up yet; she couldn't have left for work already. Phoebe isn't sure what day of the week it is. The air smells musty, as though the windows haven't been opened for a few days. She didn't think to look for Alice's car in the parking lot.

She picks herself up from the carpet and closes the window. The rooms are silent as the grave except for the faint tock of the clock in the living room. She walks down the hall and peers into the empty bathroom. There's no one in the living room, no one in the kitchen. She opens the refrigerator to stare at the contents. Skim milk. No beer. A half loaf of white bread. She looks in the cupboard for the bag of chips she was working on before she left. She wanders back through the apartment, hungry and wondering where the hell Alice has gone off to.

She returns to the living room to turn on the TV. Nothing on but farm news and a preacher, so she settles for farm news. Phoebe pulls a plastic bag from the pocket of her black leather jacket and sifts a little of the contents into a cigarette paper. Expertly, she rolls herself a joint. She watches the farm report through a haze of smoke, then a rerun of *The Dukes of Hazzard,* then a couple of news shows with talking heads.

Around about noon, she starts making calls. "Spike? Phoebe. Wake up, man. It ain't early, it's late. I'm still up. I'm having a party tonight. Shee-ut, you don't need to work tomorrow. You can call in sick. Got any crank? Yeah, black beauties will do. Bring anything that'll keep me awake."

She dials another number. "Hey, sweet girl," she says softly. "It's me. I found us a little place where we can be by ourselves. Why don't you stop by this evening? Can you bring beer?"

She leaves the next message on an answering machine. "Buddy. This is Phoebe. I want to see you again. Tonight."

Phoebe makes calls and smokes reefer and watches TV until she dozes off in the middle of a car chase. She's awakened after dark by the pounding of the first guest's fist on the door.

CARLA'S BOXES HAVE GONE beyond rectangles. For this last box of Phoebe, she's built a scale model of Alice's apartment: the single bedroom at the end of the hallway, the bathroom, the living room, the kitchen. She works on the decorations and furnishings, the clock on the wall, the writing table in the bedroom, until it's like a dollhouse. When she has every detail complete, she rummages around in the paper bags of plastic people that Frederico brought her and brings out handfuls of creatures: cowboys and cowgirls, muscular bearded men, sinuous snakelike women. She makes a great pile of them and, one by one, she manages to fit all of them into the connected boxes of the apartment. Phoebe is on the bed, entwined with more than one person. An amorous couple is in the corner. A few figures are passed out on the floor. The rest of the rooms are jammed with figures leaning against the walls or against each other, smoking tiny cigarettes, drinking from tiny cans. Several naked people wriggle in the bathtub. In the living room, a man shoots cardboard flames from his mouth. One of the windows is broken out. On the roof of the apartment, a woman howls at the moon; her arms are stretched toward the sky. Carla expands the scenery outside to include angry neighbors poking their heads out of windows and a police car speeding down the road nearby.

Carla has put a red lightbulb from a Christmas tree inside Phoebe's box so that it glows like an ember atop the table. She begins another box next to it. She works on it all night. When the light outside her windows is grey, and she is done, she smiles down at her creation and encircles the box with her arms like a beneficent goddess.

AGAINST MY WILL, SORT OF, I lay down on Morgan's cot. I was so tired. I woke to see the sky turning a purplish blue outside the window. Morgan's bed was arranged so she could see the sky when she lay there. I gazed at the tumbling clouds lit by the last bit of sunset. The tops of the trees were barely moving, but the wind must have been much stronger above them. The clouds changed form as though they were alive.

Morgan was over by the sink, messing around with dishes. "Hi," she smiled when she saw my eyes were open.

"Wow. I slept forever."

"Almost," she said.

"You haven't been here the whole time, have you?"

"Oh, no, I've been in and out."

"Taking scary pictures?"

"No scary pictures today," she said. "Did you have any dreams?"

"I'm not much of a dreamer," I said. "All I ever dream about is something chasing me."

She came over to the bed and sat down next to my pillow. "I think you dream. You talk in your sleep."

"Do I snore too?"

"A little."

"What did I say?"

"Nothing I could understand. It sounded like glossolalia."

With Morgan sitting so close to my head, I could smell the spice of her perfume. She stroked my hair, and I felt a rush of lust I hadn't experienced since Beatrice. "Come here," I said, and pulled her to me.

In the faint light, our shadows played against the wall next to the bed. I couldn't tell whose shadow belonged to whom. When it's your first time with another woman, there are surprises and recognitions. Morgan's body was both new and familiar to me—warm at the base of her spine, cooler up toward her shoulders. We navigated each other like explorers. I traced the outline of her back and breasts and thought about the pictures on the other side of the studio door that entwined beauty and terror. I was glad to be risking my life with her.

I made it my mission to kiss every inch of her skin. Morgan had a dark line of hair that extended from her belly to between her legs. I followed that line with my tongue. No angels watched over us as we made love.

Later, Morgan's voice from the darkness asked, "Have you ever flown at night?"

"No." I noticed my arms were faintly glowing.

"It's interesting," she said. "The stars overhead make you feel like you can rise forever."

"How high up have you gone?"

"Only as high as the geese. I still need to breathe, like they do."

I sat up and pulled the pack of cigarettes from my shirt pocket. "Is it okay if I smoke inside?" I asked.

"Can I have one?"

Finally, someone who didn't emanate self-righteousness every time I lit up. I lit two cigarettes and passed one to her. Our fingers just brushed. I could see the glowing tip of her cigarette as it rose and fell in the darkness of the studio. I love the smell of cigarette smoke.

"We should fly tonight," Morgan said.

"Tonight?" The idea of flying in the dark scared me.

"Why not? The wind makes it more fun."

I worried about getting lost. Should one pack navigational instruments when embarking on a celestial journey? We finished our cigarettes.

"Let's go," she said.

We went out the back door so we wouldn't be seen and stood next to a dumpster. It was so late the street was empty and silent. We could still hear the sirens faintly from where we stood. The ugly strip mall where Morgan lived and worked was transformed by the night into cold beauty, a place of mystery whose secrets lay behind its cheap walls and in its empty places.

We rose in unison, silently up and up and up, above the street, above the tobacco warehouses a mile away, slowly up and up and up until we were hovering just under the great dark dome of the sky, the stars closer to us now than the tiny lights of the land below. I was at the very edge of what I could do; I was where I was not supposed to be.

Orion danced on the horizon. The clarity of the night revealed that there was no heaven above us, only stars too far away to ever reach, stars that shone incessantly. You could make yourself believe in a heaven above the blue vault of day, but at night you could plainly see that there was nothing there. I could still hear the note though, even louder. It must have been the music of the unknowing and enormous spheres. My arms were plainly glowing now in the dark night.

I heard Morgan laugh. She was further away than I had thought. The starlight wasn't enough to let me see her, just the impression of her dark form. The celestial spheres ground out their unceasing tone. The black trees below us whipped in the wind. The wind blew harder, as if trying to blow us out of the sky and back onto the ground where we belonged.

She flew close to me. I could feel the warmth of her body through the coldness of the night. Far away, I thought I could hear the roar of waves crashing. They sounded like the wind. "Let's go to the ocean," I shouted over the wind. Her dark silhouette nodded and started toward the east. I followed her, losing sight of her and finding her again. "Wait!" I called, but she didn't hear me.

I glanced down at the land so far below me. I could see what Morgan saw: the river of light that must have been the interstate, the bright flower of a building on fire that was beautiful in the dark night. I heard voices from the earth that were raised in joy or terror, I was too far away to tell. We flew over forests silent except for the calls of owls. We flew beyond the shore over the roiling dark waters. The stars swung in their courses above us. Seagulls cried all around me, sounding like voices from the earth.

"Morgan?" I called out. I couldn't see her. She grabbed my hand. Then it was the two of us, floating together above the dark sphere of the earth. I did not know what kept us from spinning off into the space out among the stars.

From our place so high above the ocean, we saw the eastern sky brighten and light the great circle of the watery horizon below it. I reached out with my glowing hand to touch Morgan's halo of hair. Just before daybreak, just before the light, I heard the beat of angels' wings. I saw a ring of fire.

Firebrand Books is an award-winning feminist and lesbian publishing house. We are committed to producing quality work in a wide variety of genres by ethnically and racially diverse authors. Now in our fourteenth year, we have over ninety titles in print.

A free catalog is available on request from Firebrand Books, 141 The Commons, Ithaca, New York 14850, (607) 272-0000.

Visit our website at www.firebrandbooks.com